Colorful
Notions

I0691473

Colorful Notions

THE ROADTRIPPERS 1.0

Mohit Goyal

Srishti
PUBLISHERS & DISTRIBUTORS

SRISHTI PUBLISHERS & DISTRIBUTORS
Registered Office: N-16, C.R. Park
New Delhi – 110 019
Corporate Office: 212A, Peacock Lane
Shahpur Jat, New Delhi – 110 049
editorial@srishtipublishers.com

First published by
Srishti Publishers & Distributors in 2017

Copyright © Mohit Goyal, 2017

10 9 8 7 6 5 4 3 2 1

This is a work of fiction. The characters, places, organisations and events described in this book are either a work of the author's imagination or have been used fictitiously. Any resemblance to people, living or dead, places, events, communities or organisations is purely coincidental.

The author asserts the moral right to be identified as the author of this work.

All rights reserved. No part of this publication may be reproduced, stored in a retrieval system, or transmitted, in any form or by any means, electronic, mechanical, photocopying, recording or otherwise, without the prior written permission of the Publishers.

To all under-privileged, orphaned or disadvantaged children…
…They too deserve to read, to eat healthy,
They too deserve to get all the love,
They too deserve their childhood

I pledge to give away proceeds from this book to
CRY – Child Rights and You.

CRY is an Indian NGO that believes in every child's
right to a childhood – to live, learn, grow and play.
For over 30 years, CRY and its 200 partner NGOs
have worked with parents and communities to
ensure lasting change in the lives of more
than 20,00,000 underprivileged children,
across 23 states in India.

www.cry.org

Ensuring lasting change
for children

No more regrets.
No turning back. This is it.

"**I**ndia isn't as simple a country as you think it is. You can't drive safely at odd hours. Roads are bumpy. You will be staying at lodges with the sounds of passing trucks all night. And don't even think about the number of times your car will break down throughout the journey. Don't even get me started on that. In short, it's a crazy idea straight out of Bollywood!"

"But uncle, that's precisely what we are setting out to do. I want to have a roadtripping experience that I can record and also make a movie out of!" I said candidly. I knew I had overdone myself here. I mean, a real movie? Like really?

"And," Sashank said, "Mama, imagine the sumptuous food we are going to get dirty on!"

Food was always on his mind. Uncle stared at him.

That's Sashank, our Sasha, for you. He thinks food, sleeps food and lives food. Celebrated writer George Bernard Shaw once said, "There is no sincerer love than the love for food." My poor little friend took it way too seriously.

Then, it helped that he had an equally crazy (if not more) BFF in me, Abhay or Ab. BFF is our new-age term for chaddi-buddies by the way; something you'd associate with Laurel and Hardy in history, or Jai-Veeru, or Amar-Prem, or Munna-Circuit from the movies.

I hadn't found my bliss in life yet, unlike my foodie friend, but I never gave up trying. Making a docu-movie on travel had been a dream I had been nurturing ever since I had watched travel shows like *Indian Holiday* by Mini Mathur as a child. It's a different matter that like most things in life, which we fantasize about, this one also took a backseat.

But now I was adamant about doing it. If completed, it would be the first milestone I'd ever achieve in my life. Buoyed by my friend's passion for food and trying out new cuisines, we somehow married our goals to each other's.

Sasha announced to his ever-flourishing joint family of sixteen that he'd be taking a sabbatical from their trading business for a three month long adventure. Not that they complained, considering the number of hands that were already running the well-settled business. Yet, his worried mother packed the two of us to her brother, an avid traveler himself, for some counseling and instilling sense.

I never had such problems, mainly because of my rich divorced parents who lived in different homes. For a while, I tried to stay with my father and his new partner after I graduated. But it became increasingly difficult to bear the strangeness of seeing him with someone else. I decided to move out quietly. But, he felt guilty for my state and kept depositing hefty sums in my bank account every month. Long-story-short, I was on my own when it came to decisions about my life, and so I just resigned from my present job in the advertising agency and began planning this odyssey.

But first, our task was to encounter this session with uncle.

"Okay, which places do you want to go to?" he asked, sensing that we were pretty serious. I could read him buying into our idea.

"Uncle, we will be going to twenty-five places across the length and breadth of the country!" I said.

"Twenty-five? Why twenty-five?"

We looked at each other and grinned because of the relevance and familiarity of his question. Initially, we had argued a lot over many beers about the number of places we would go to.

We couldn't think of a fair number of places that could count as 'covering the entire country' even after a lot of research. We chose something symbolic, i.e., twenty-five as our target number because we were both in our twenty-fifth years in life. I had celebrated by twenty-fifth birthday already, but Sasha's was a few months away.

We both thought it would be cool to say that we had gone on a road trip to twenty-five places together to mark our friendship and turning twenty-five! In Sasha's case, it was more about the different cuisines and types of cooking he would have tried.

"Come on, talk to me kids!"

"You will think of our reason as childish," I said, hoping that making it sound mysterious will make it nobler than it really was. I then added for effect, "But these twenty-five places represent our country's culture, heritage and beauty. We intend to go to places as religious as Jagannath Puri and as raunchy as the beach parties in Goa!"

Sasha didn't like my mentioning beach parties. He knew about my carelessness with words. I never had to be accountable to anyone. But since Sasha was brought up in a protective environment, he was wary about giving away too many details. Luckily, his uncle was cool. Perhaps because he was a traveler himself. I could see it in his eyes as he started recounting his travel stories. He went on and on, and after some half-an-hour of a one-sided conversation, where he talked and we listened, I interrupted him.

"Here's our list, uncle." I handed him a piece of paper.

Start Point: New Delhi

(1)	Corbett Park	230 km
(2)	Haridwar	150 km
(3)	Rishikesh	40 km
(4,5)	Manali and Ladakh	950 km
(6)	Wagah Border and Golden Temple, Amritsar	850 km
(7)	Bhangarh Fort, Alwar	550 km
(8)	Pink City, Jaipur and Chokhi Dhani	150 km
(9)	Thar Dessert, Jaisalmer	550 km
(10)	Hiking in Mount Abu	450 km

(11)	Lake Pichola, Udaipur	150 km
(12)	Rann of Kutch	650 km
(13)	Ellora Caves	950 km
(14)	Beaches of Goa	200 km
(15)	Mysore	100 km
(16)	Kanyakumari	80 km
(17)	Temples of Rameshwaram	300 km
(18)	Hyderabad	1100 km
(19)	Jagannath Puri	1000 km
(20,21)	Kolkata, Sundarbans	500 km
(22)	Bodhgaya, Bihar	650 km
(23)	Ghats of Varanasi	250 km
(24)	Taj Mahal, Agra	600 km
(25)	Jama Masjid, Delhi	200 km

"You boys have really thought it out!" He was clearly astonished. Then he cautioned us. "Do you have any idea how much travel it is going to involve? I'd imagine ten thousand kilometers at least! Maybe more. It's your job to find out, but you really will go bananas with that much driving!"

"To be precise, 10,650 kilometers. With ten hours of driving time, or 350-400 kilometers per day, we will be driving for around thirty days throughout the trip and halting and staying for another thirty or forty-five days. A total of seventy-five days, and we will cover the entire country!"

"Suck the maths Abhay, it's going to be rough!" He smirked.

"Mama, we'll manage, it's a once-in-a-lifetime experience. Please let us do it!" Sasha begged. He knew that without mama's approval, his mother might not support the trip at all.

"I am not saying that you shouldn't go! I am just making sure you are aware of the hardships and consequences, that's all!"

I said, "Nothing will go wrong, uncle, trust me. We are going to take my SUV and will drive by turn. At best, we will extend the trip by a few days to make sure that we aren't dead from all that driving."

"Okay, okay! Go home, you two. Start planning. I will call your mom and tell her it's safe for you to go. Send me a message or an email every few days. Keep updating her about your whereabouts as well. By the way, Abhay, how are you going to record it? I mean, you said you are going to make a movie!" he asked.

"Yes uncle, I will take my camera along and record everything. I will shoot the places, and talk to the locals, videograph the food and even portions of our journey."

"That's it? Won't it be a little boring for anyone to watch it this way?"

"Why boring uncle? We will stick to popular destinations that people like to go to. You know, places like Rajasthan, Goa, Kerala, etc. This isn't for unconventional tourism, but mainstream one only. It does make an exciting watch!"

Uncle still looked concerned. "Actually, err uncle," I looked at Sasha, looking for his approval first. He looked away. I didn't know what to do, so I blurted out, "Sashank's friend, a radio jockey is going to join us. She will be doing the voice-over, as though delivering a running commentary for all that we see—"

He cut me short. "You are going to take girls along? Watch it, boys. It's a big responsibility. You know what I mean. Who is she? Sashank, do you have a girlfriend?" Sasha had no answer.

Though he was my best friend since childhood, I couldn't lie about his looks or his charisma. He has very little in both departments. I guess that's why his mama was surprised.

"No, uncle! Not going around. They are good friends," I said on his behalf.

"Relax boys, I know what 'good friends' are. I was the cool one in the family. No need to worry about me, but make sure you give the right information to his mother. Remember Sashank, how we went on that trip to Damdama Lake last year and found an old friend of mine? While my wife was okay, both your parents were staring at her rather disgusted!" Then, he went on and on about the incident that Sasha seemed to have little clue about.

Again I had to butt in. "So, uncle, we have your blessings for our trip?"

He smiled and nodded. We bid him goodbye. At least one of our problems was over. I wondered if my friend was really going to be twenty-five. I mean, why couldn't a twenty-five-year-old decide to stay alone for a few months? I had been living like this for years. The next task was to convince Unnati's parents. Unnati was the girl Sasha was seeing, and also the major, major protagonist of our story.

❖

"Get out of my room, you bitch!" A loud voice sounded. It wasn't the kind of welcome we were expecting. We wondered what to do next. Just then, there came a louder voice, probably in response, "Stop swearing, Timki! Look at you! The language you've picked up! I am going to complain to Mom." Unnati stepped out of the door, standing right there in her nightwear or something and looked hot.

Even though her jawline was slightly protruding, showing more of her front teeth than necessary, to put it politely; the rest of her body features were as perfect as they come. I mean, yeah she was my best friend's girl and all, but no harm in a bit of admiration, right? Sometimes, in fact, I really wondered how my food-obsessed friend scored with this chic. But let's save it for another day.

Unnati hugged Sashank. I smiled. After exchanging pleasantries, we went into the drawing room and waited for her folks. Her mom arrived wearing a very short dress and too much make-up.

"Hello a auntyji," Sasha was polite, speaking with folded hands like an ideal prospective son-in-law should. He bent forward as though to touch her feet, seeking her blessings. She extended her hands and hugged him, pressing him into her bosom.

"No need, mere bachche. You are my son, after all. Come, sit!" He followed her to the sofa in the huge living room. I was neither the 'son', nor did I take her blessing, but I chose to sit with them quietly. Unnati introduced me, saying, "Mom, this is Abhay. Sasha's childhood friend."

Her mom stared at me, "Oh, so you are the producer! God bless you, bachche. You are so young! Learn something from him, you two!"

I guess they had talked me up to her. I mean, besides contributing my car and the camera, I was bringing nothing to the table. But I didn't mind this adulation.

"Aunty, I am not a big time one. But yeah, this documentary-movie will be big, I assure you. I have contacts, good contacts. We will even get a satellite release later!"

Sasha looked at me with his mouth half-open. Of course, I am bull shitting, you moron!

Aunty was impressed. She said, "But bachche, I am still not happy about Unnati going alone for three months like this. Though I am modern, her father will get very angry if I tell him that Unnati is traveling alone with two boys."

Sasha was silent. Once again, I lied. "Aunty, don't worry about her being alone. I've arranged for some local crew at various places, both girls and boys. She is the star of the film, from the first to the last shot. That's why she has to travel everywhere. Please understand. Can you imagine *Hum Aapke Hain Kaun* without Madhuri Dixit?"

Though her eyes lit up, she wasn't fully convinced. "I will talk to your papa, let's see what he says about this. Of course, I have no objection considering that you already talk nonsense on your radio channel all day. This sounds a lot better than that!" she told Unnati and then began to get up.

As she left, Unnati was the first to laugh. "Me? Like Madhuri Dixit? You really blew this up big time, Abhay!" She laughed and punched me in the arm.

Sasha said, "What difference does it make, yaar? Aunty still doesn't look convinced." He helped himself to a few more cookies.

"No, she is. You know her secret desire was to become a movie star. The way Abhay described the road-trip, I am sure she will be happy if her daughter can fulfill her ambition, even if partly."

She started laughing again. "I am saying that she is convinced already. My dad just can't say no now. Yay!" She started celebrating, jumping up and down on the sofa. Sasha joined in the fun.

I started wondering if I was their alter-parent or something. The previous day I met Sashank's uncle and got him onboard. It was Unnati's mother next. They both seemed to be depending on my story here.

My story? What's my real story? I mean, if I just wanted to travel, I can tank-up my car and go. Why do I need these overgrown kids to come along? I knew all along that their parents would probably think they were out to make a movie while he actually will be busy eating. His girl will seek out romantic locations...

I have been a loner all my life. Then why do I need them on my adventure? Was it due to my own insecurities that I'd never be able to do it? Or that I wanted somebody in my odyssey for company's sake? Or something else?

I looked at Sasha. His face smeared with coffee froth, weight inversely proportional to his height and a balding head – the guy was still my best friend. He had been around for a long, long time. Probably he needed this break to discover himself, he needed me as an anchor.

And then I looked at his girlfriend. Even though I couldn't stop wondering again how he got her, she looked as clueless about life as him. I mean, being an Assistant RJ at twenty-five? Most girls her age are better settled in their lives.

We decided to begin our journey on 1 April. It was a couple of weeks away. It was going to get terribly hot in most parts of India, but we couldn't choose colder weather since it would have limited our access to some omissible spots. Also, 1 April seemed apt, given our crazy plan, to the point of sounding foolish to others. We had a huge pile of things to do – buying equipment for shooting, camping, all kinds of clothing, making as many advance reservations as we possibly could, planning route maps and then re-planning their backups, to name a few. The wisest way to do this was to divide our tasks, which we did.

The most important thing to be done was getting my car ready. It was a road trip after all. It was our top resource. Even though I was proud of it, I couldn't help stare at my 2010 mini-SUV EcoSport and wonder if the car would make it, could really take that much load.

The car had been with me for three years now. It had survived many trips to Moorthal and Meerut and two or three overnight escapades. It had escaped unhurt mostly.

But this was to be an acid test for my Little Beast, as Sasha called it. To be driven around for over ten thousand kilometers without much rest was no mean task. Add to it the extreme conditions of our highways and small-town roads.

Owing to financial limitations, we had to settle with what we had. With the fuel, hotel bookings and so much food (read, Sasha's appetite was bigger than Unnati's and mine put together) and other miscellaneous costs that were staring us, we couldn't afford the luxury of a better car.

We met for the final time before the trip on 31 March. In the evening, we dumped all the stuff we had packed into the boot of the car. We made ten to twelve pouches of cash, comprising five thousand rupees each, and hid them in what we thought were secret places, including the beast's tool kit, the first aid box, a small hole in rear seat's upholstery, under a particular carpet mat and even one inside the front engine, near the coolant jar.

Our idea was to have little cash and cards on our person, as we were going to stay at unknown places. It never hurts to be extra careful. There were locations where there were no swipe machines or ATMs. In short, the three of us felt our physical preparation to be as complete as they could be. But it didn't mean we could sleep well that night. Sometimes when you are so close to what you have been dreaming of, you have this tendency of rechecking whether or not you have it in you.

I guess Sasha also felt it; he called me at one in the morning. "Bhai, all set for tomorrow?"

"Yeah, bhai! Why, did we miss out something?"

"I don't know man, what is to be done now?"

I tried to sound confident. "What do you mean what is to be done now? Get up at 6:00 a.m. and start. We can't back out now!"

"No, you got me wrong. I was just thinking. Why did we choose so many places? Shouldn't we have cut down our list to about twelve or thirteen real good places? Come on, we have been to the Taj Mahal and Chowki Dhani already…"

I cut him short, "Sashank Gupta, it's too late to make any changes whatsoever. Besides, we have already talked about this, no? We agreed that Jaipur is worth being called the cultural capital of India. And how can any travel expedition in India ever be considered complete without visiting the Taj? That's why we kept it as the penultimate destination. Bhai, don't get nervous now!"

He still was skeptical. "Okay, okay. But do we really need to travel so far all the way to Ladakh? What if we connect straight from Rishikesh to Amritsar? Won't we be saving over a thousand kilometers of travel!"

"You are missing the point, Sasha. We don't need to travel so far. Let's just visit the Select City Walk Mall in Saket and come back home. Just twenty kilometers. That's all it will take. You can eat good food there, too."

His voice rose, "Why do you keep bringing food into every conversation, yaar? This trip isn't only about food. It is a journey, a travelogue that encompasses our entire country."

"Exactly!"

No more words were exchanged. My friend isn't as silly as I sometimes may project him (throughout this book). He hung up after a few silly smirks over differences between Kashmiri girls and Punjabi ones. We finally slept off and decided to meet at his house at 6:15 a.m. the next morning before we proceeded to pick up Unnati.

Don't always look for danger

Being an amateur cameraman, I had stared at many sunrises in the past. I had been to many beaches in south Goa just to shoot the sunrise. It was beautiful how a murky blue haze over the sea slowly turned into dark orange and then into a bright blue. I once went on a pilgrimage to Haridwar, specifically to the ghats, to shoot the sunrise. The ghats were peaceful in the morning, but turned noisy as the day progressed.

That morning had no such eccentric features, yet it stood out in a meditative way. Staring into the brightness and waiting outside Sasha's home, I closed my eyes reminding myself of how I had wanted this sojourn for a very long time, living like a nomad.

Sashank came out with two plastic cups. We didn't talk, just sipped our coffee and drove to Unnati's place. Her parents were outside to see her off. They hugged her tight and wished us well, reminding us of our responsibilities towards them, the female traveler, our parents, society and even our country! Finally, our journey started. Even though the three musketeers wouldn't be an exact description, we still hummed 'All for One and One for All' from the movie to mark our beginning.

"Do we stop for breakfast?" Unnati asked from the back seat.

"Nope!"

"But I am starving!" We turned around and looked at her. She had her hands on her stomach already.

"Let us travel a quick distance and beat the Delhi traffic first, Unnati. We are hitting NH 24 in an hour or so. Then, we can stop at a roadside dhaba."

Then I continued, "Listen up, girl. Our first stopover shall also be our first recording site. Be prepared with your make-up and whatever. And remember, you have to speak impromptu."

Just as we left the city, there was a long array of roadside food joints. Sasha said, "Let me decide which to choose; it is my domain after all. Ladies and…"

I interrupted him, "Wait, let me capture this." I slowed the car down and switched my camera on, pointing at him. "Action!"

"Ladies and gentlemen, I thank you for joining us on this amazing, amazing journey. Let me assure you that this will be a mind-numbing experience; memories that all of us will carry to our graves. These three months will have a lot of action, drama, fun, and most of all – adventure. But to do all that, we all need fuel in our bodies. I will be your host, your navigator who presents the best of local cuisines and delicacies to you, to make sure we return home healthier than we left. While my friend here," he pointed at Unnati, "will be lending her sweet voice-over as we go about our journey. Say hi, Unnati!"

I turned the camera to focus on her. She blew flying kisses and smiled. Then the camera focused on Sasha again as he continued. "And behind the camera is our captain of the ship, Abhay Mathur, who is also the director, cameraman, editor, producer and even the spot boy!"

"Thanks!" I said curtly, pointing the camera back at myself. "Now, our very first stopover meal shall bring the best of our food heritage! This is something all us kids of North India grew up eating – paranthas. Yes, AB my friend! Park the car to your right at 'Punjabi Rasoi'. Let's get lost in the delightful world of buttered paranthas. Statutory warning: you won't be able to leave without dirtying your hands and soul-orgasmic feeling."

I stopped at that very moment. "Cut it Sasha, guys this is going to be a serious film!"

He just tapped my arm lightly and said, "What dude? It is Unnati's job anyway. You will edit me out later, I know very well!"

But Unnati bent forward and kissed him on his right cheek. "No my coochie, you spoke so nicely!"

I sighed and parked the car outside Punjabi Rasoi. I must admit as I stepped out, this was by far the best looking set-up amidst the horde of restaurants in the vicinity. We gorged on some delicious aloo and gobhi paranthas and gulped down tall glasses of lassi. Sasha liked them so much that he got a few of them packed, 'just in case' we needed them. After a breakfast that'd do Kumbhkaran proud, I set up my camera on a stand outside and Unnati stood with a mic.

"The weather is absolutely beautiful. What a perfect start to our journey! This stop is worth remem..." She had barely spoken a few words when a crowd gathered around us.

"What are you shooting for?"

"Which film?"

"Who is this new heroine? What's her name?"

There were all sorts of questions. I noticed Sasha even talking to a cook, "Heroine is new but so what, our director saab is an old pro. See behind that camera!" pointing at me. "Discount *to doge na, bhaiya...*"

I wondered how difficult it must be for someone like Karan Johar in this country. No wonder that they erect artificial sets.

"Pack up!" I said. I decided we would rather shoot our introduction somewhere else or just do a voice-over.

Leaving an unpaid bill, with speculations over the likely super-hit Bollywood film behind, we made our way to our first destination – the Jim Corbett National Park. On Day 1,we did not have much road to travel and reached Kashipur in less than three hours.

My friends were impatient. "Speed up AB! If we are there before noon, we can go for the jeep safari. Then there is a better chance to catch a tiger!" Sashank said.

"Whoaa! Did you say tiger? I heard you can only spot a tiger in Corbett on YouTube!" said Unnati. She was visiting Corbett for the third or fourth time and claimed that she had never seen any animal other than deer or wild boars. Sasha wasn't impressed. "This is a grand adventure. You see how tigers will indeed honor us and make a visit."

"Sasha... If a tiger really comes and I get scared, will you save me?" she asked, sounding mushy and girlie.

This time I replied, "Yeah, don't worry, Unnati. Sasha saves all the food for himself!" I winked at Sasha. Unnati didn't get the joke so settled back on the seat.

Soon, our destination was in sight. 'Jim Corbett National Park,' said the signboard. We stopped our car outside to take pictures.

We had brought along (I forgot to mention earlier), numeric signs from 1 to 25 and had to take some selfies as we went about each of those respective destinations. The three of us huddled together making faces and Sasha held no '1' in the middle as I clicked our first picture. Now I can tell you, but we didn't know then that these number-placards were to play a very crucial role in saving our butts.

The stay was to be just for a night at our first destination. After checking in at a lodge in Dhikala, where it was most likely to sight rare wildlife, we decided to venture out.

❖

"Mutthuraman Swaminathan Unnikrishnan, sir." His accent made obvious that he was from the South, and his name affirmed it. Here he was, a south Indian tourist guide miraculously stuck in a northern wildlife sanctuary where idli wouldn't be the easiest thing to find on menu.

"Sir, how do we call you?" I asked him as politely as I could.

"No... No need to call me sir, sir. Call me Unni. Better."

"Okay Unni... bhai. We want to go on a safari now."

He was happy and smiling. "You call me 'bhai'...brother. I like. You north Indians all call each other 'bhai'. I feel good. Let's go sir, we go now. I show you elephant – very nice. I show you so many animal, you feel double nice."

"Unni bhai, we see so many animal already. Now, madam want to see tiger, can you show?" Sasha said pointing to Unnati.

"Madam wants to see a tiger? Then I will show you a tiger. But one condition. I will take my car. Jeep. Not park's. My jeep can go everywhere, wherever the tiger comes to rest, to sleep, and to do susu-potty."

"Okay okay."

"My car, extra charge, sir. Three thousand rupees."

I looked at Sasha and gestured to him with my eyes to find another guide. But Unni wasn't going to give up easily. "I know you think Unni is charging so high. The listed rate is 2000. But you have come to shoot with a camera, right? Sir, Unni knows all the places where you can shoot. I even will also show you a tiger eating a bull's flesh!"

His pitch was clearly to me as he spotted the equipment. I was won over. A tiger feasting will definitely be the rarest of rare sights for any film. After some negotiation over his fees, we agreed. We had a quick lunch at the 'Jungle Retreat' restaurant that had deer faces on its walls and no non-vegetarian food on its menu. We then went towards his jeep.

"Dude, this guy is a good catch, totally our type!" Sasha said as we walked.

"Why do you think so?"

"Look at him sipping from his water bottle. It's liquor, man. We will have a good time inside, it is otherwise prohibited to drink during a safari!"

I wasn't sure. But the prospect of capturing pictures of a tiger eating its supper overpowered everything else. We settled into the uncomfortable open jeep. Sasha was in front with Unni at the driver's seat. I sat behind with Unnati and set up the camera, focusing on her as she spoke. She looked pretty, I have to say.

We had hardly travelled for half-an-hour when he stopped his jeep. There were no other cars on that road. Unni stepped down silently, clearly against the rules. He signaled to us to remain seated. He walked a couple of steps into the bushes without breaking into a sweat. This seemed like core area and the guide's confidence before we engaged him meant that we really were onto something here. I was thrilled, though Unnati seemed scared. It's one thing to imagine seeing a tiger and another thing to encounter him in real! Unni waved at us, gesturing to us to get off the jeep. Sasha was unsure, but I was out in a flash, with my camera in position. I tiptoed towards the bushes. It was as silent as a jungle could be expected to be, and the only sound was that of birds chirping very swiftly.

Suddenly he thrust his full palm in the air, certainly asking us to stop in our tracks. There was complete silence for the next few minutes. All of a sudden, it felt like those birds chirping right above us had gathered steam and their noises moved in another direction.

I saw Unni running backwards to me. I froze instantly, expecting gigantic teeth to appear from somewhere and cut me into two pieces.

But he ran straight to his jeep and shouted, "Sir, let's go! Thetiger is right ahead."

I was frozen to the spot but saw Sasha waving at me, asking me to get into the jeep. I jumped into the jeep, thanking all the gods whose names I knew.

We drove quickly and parked under a tree. This time Unni didn't step out, probably anticipating the king-of-the-jungle to appear. We heard strange noises after a while and positioned our cameras and binoculars. Sasha whispered to Unnati, "Baby, are you scared?"

Her voice hardly came out in the affirmative. Then, she slowly said, "AB, let's go. There is no tiger here."

Unni hushed us. The birds flocked together once again and cried loudly. Now I was no wildlife specialist, but it certainly meant some action somewhere close to us. Just then, there was a sound of a car behind. And then another. Within a matter of seconds, there were three more cars parked. Their guides sat up in their seats in anticipation, and chatted in sign language with Unni. Nobody in those cars moved an inch. It was as if the entire world had chosen to be silent, just to catch a glimpse of the carnivorous animal.

Suddenly, the guides started pointing in a direction where some bushes moved swiftly. "There, there!" one of them shouted in delight to his group. We stared in that direction. I had my camera ready to capture all this excitement. Some people from another car pointed and clearly seemed to have spotted the tiger, while the three of us just kept staring blankly at the bushes and then at each other. This continued for another ten minutes, after which, the guides unanimously decided that the tiger had left the spot. After congratulating each other, they left to drive their respective cars. Unni turned to us with a huge smile, "Did you see sir? I told you Unni is a genius!"

I expected my friends to counter him. But no one said anything. If the guides had seen him, and the rest of the groups apparently saw him, too...how could we admit to not seeing anything?

"Abhay sir, hope you got a good picture!" Unni said.

"Yeah! Thanks Unni!" I lied to play along. After that, Unni was full of confidence. We saw other wildlife and some scenic beauty during the rest of our safari. Here was a guide, who rarely missed out on showing tigers to his customers. We noticed that his drinking speed had increased. The guy was on his own rejoicing trip after that as we drove for another couple of hours.

That evening, we decided that it was better to stay indoors and have a quiet meal. Although I had decided to get some good voiceovers from Unnati in Corbett's backdrop, I had to reserve them for later. We had a quiet dinner and decided to put a full stop to our first action-packed day. I retired to my room and viewed the raw footage of our shoot since the morning. I mentally prepared to edit and project the film so far and then drifted off to sleep.

Kumbh madness and reminiscences

We checked out from the lodge early enough to prompt the manager to ask us if we didn't like our stay.

Sasha told him, "No no, it was very good. We have a long journey ahead, that's all."

"Any luck in the jungle, sir?"

"Yeah, we saw a tiger!" Sasha said and winked at me. I should have clarified it with him, then.

"My god! You're so lucky. I have not heard of any tourist spotting a tiger in a long while!" he was beaming at our good luck.

I chipped in, "I could have almost been killed when I got off the jeep."

The manager laughed. Then, almost as if to assure us, he said, "Never heard of that before either, sir! Don't worry. Animals don't attack till they are provoked. Man is a bigger threat."

I guess Sasha liked what he said. He lightened up and changed the topic. "Boss, the jungle is so thanda. No alcohol, or even beer. What man! I am never coming back."

Now, the manager was offended and took it as his responsibility to safeguard Corbett tourism. He asked us to come to a room at the back, and showed us a good collection of rum, scotch and beer. Sasha and I drooled at the sight.

"Sir, we have 'everything' here discreetly. The park doesn't allow it, but we know guests are here for a good time. But please, don't drink when you are on the safari!" he said, rubbing his palms.

"Don't worry, buddy. We are leaving. Do you mind if I take some cans of beer?" I asked him.

"This is for you only!" He handed us a vacuum packed case of six Budweiser cans. "That will be a thousand rupees, sir!"

This time it was our turn to be offended. "What?" I whispered in his ear. "Let's go! We can get some from Ramnagar."

"Sir, it is strictly prohibited here. We sneak it in!" Sasha quietly handed him a thousand-rupee note. He was too delighted to miss having beer and too eager to get out than negotiate. At 8:30 a.m., when the rest of the world must be sipping their tea, Sasha and I sat in the Beast, drinking beer.

Just then, Unnati came with her backpack and opened the backdoor. "Are you guys nuts?" she shouted at us. We just looked at her, and went back to our cans. I guess when the argument is between choosing wine and women, the former wins. She just shook her head and slipped into the backseat.

"Don't drink too much AB, or else I will have to drive!" she warned, only to be ignored again as I switched on the engine.

The distance from Corbett to Haridwar, our next destination was a short 100-120 kilometers or so, and would take us about two hours. We kept it a little easy for the first few days so that we could warm up to the long tour ahead of us. There wasn't much to do in Haridwar, except to crash at some never-tried-before food joints and shoot the late evening or early morning sights of the Ganga. We timed our visit to the sacred city when the Kumbh Mela was on. Considered the largest pilgrimage and among the most peaceful gatherings in the world, it is held once every three years in rotation at four different cities, on the banks of sacred rivers. Talking about such a sanctified event with beer in my veins is a real crime; but we had planned to land up in Haridwar at a time when the Kumbh Mela was being hosted there. Though none of us was exactly religious, we thought it would be nice to check out the event. Capturing the largest human gathering in my film was another temptation.

NH 74 led to Haridwar. It wasn't particularly driver-friendly. Cattle appeared at random and straight out of nowhere. At last, we had to stop for a while when Unnati complained that she was not drinking anything while her boyfriend had emptied four cans of crucifying-water! We stopped by a roadside vendor selling sugarcane juice.

Unnati got off, turning heads in that small-town market. Wearing a bright red short-sleeve top with a muffler around her neck, I must admit that I was leeching at my best friend's girlfriend. She asked for a huge glass of the juice. She drank out of it without letting it touch her mouth. Some of it slipped down her fair throat. I could even see some of it trickling down to her clothes, but she seemed least bothered. Too sexy if you ask me. The juice wala couldn't stop checking her out. That was when Sasha came to his senses, "Unnati, drink properly. We are not going to get a place for you to change here! Besides, don't make a scene."

She became a good girl again and finished her drink before getting back into the car.

I could see Unnati liked the extra attention she got and pulled her boyfriend's cheek to acknowledge it.

In a short while, we reached Haridwar. It was around 11:15 a.m. Haridwar was packed due to the Kumbh Mela. We had already made booking at a small inn near the ghats.

"Where do you want to take the picture guys? We are inside Haridwar already!" I asked them.

Unnati replied, "At Har ki Pauri. That is what symbolizes Haridwar no?"

"Impossible, it will be jam packed now!"

"Let's do it right here, next to that ghat where those naked sadhus are sitting. What difference will it make? You can even call it the holy Har ki Pauri ghat in your movie later, Abhay!"

Sasha was right. Alcohol makes you wise, indeed. We stopped for our customary picture, holding up a sign that said '2'. This time, we were more animated and chose to jump in the air together with our numbers flashing in front. Then, I recorded a few videos of our surroundings, while Unnati spoke in the background. "I am standing at the ghats of the sacred River Ganga, from where Haridwar is believed to begin. While early mornings offer the best view, the afternoons are equally breathtaking. It almost makes me feel meditative, just seeing these people taking a dip and saying *om-namah-shivay*. I just want to grab a chair and order chai and samosas to sit back and watch these wonderfully tranquil waters!" For a second, I really forgot that she was doing it all unrehearsed.

Our stay in Haridwar was particularly important because of Sasha's fixation with a restaurant chain called Chotiwala Restaurant. The name would ring a bell for anyone who has visited Rishikesh and Haridwar.

We landed at this place in the middle of a very busy market near Subhash Ghat. It had many imitators nearby and there was a very long queue to get inside. But my connoisseur friend cannot settle for anything less. After twenty minutes, we finally got a seat. What did we see? Sasha had already placed a big order secretly while we waited – around six to seven portions of food in different colors were laid out for us within seconds. Unnati and I looked at each other. Sasha was drowned in the visual and nasal delight! The food was delicious, no doubt, but I really wondered if it was any different from other restaurants serving North Indian vegetarian fare, or the food we had back at home. And to top it all, I could barely eat more than two rotis. Unnati had one. It meant that my hundred kilo companion gobbled the rest of it. His face brimmed with unmatchable satisfaction once he was done.

We decided to rest in our rooms in the afternoon. He deserved a long nap after eating all those calories. Since we were economy travellers, we always took two rooms, one for the boys and one for Unnati. As he dozed off, I decided to go for a walk to the ghat nearby. I had barely climbed down a couple of stairs when I spotted Unnati sitting on one of the steps, staring at the river. I walked up to her and sat beside her. After some time she said, "Why is Sashank your best friend?"

After a pause, I felt obliged to answer her, "I don't know. We've been together since childhood. We click and don't piss each other off often. Why do you ask?"

She was silent. "Did you see him all sparked up when he saw all the food laid out?"

"Yeah, food does fire him up!" I said.

"I never see that spark in him for me."

Ouch! So, my best friend's girl wanted to bitch about him. I seemed to be the chosen one. I didn't know how to handle the situation.

"So he thinks of food as something he loves to eat, and looks at you as someone he loves to be with. There is no similarity or competition. It is like, necessity versus need. Would you compare your going to a spa with your office gossip sessions?" I guess I made no sense, but it got her thinking.

"But really, Abhay, sometimes I want to be loved and pampered like other girls are. You know, my girlfriends who are married have so much to say about their romantic lives. Even the single ones who have flings! And me? My boyfriend only likes to talk about food, his bored life and crap like that. I know I am not getting any younger and may have to think of settling down soon. But I don't know what he thinks. For him, love starts and ends when we are alone and it's dark!"

Below the belt, I thought. I just didn't know how to react. There was a child in front of us, constantly trying to put his foot into the water, trying to get his parents' attention. They were about ten feet away from us, sitting like we were, soaking in the view. The child got naughtier and soon he was knee deep in the river. Just then, he lost his balance, and within the blink-of-a-second, he submerged and began struggling. His father went running. I too got up, and helped him save his son. He carried the crying child away, consoling him and thanking me.

I came back to Unnati and said, "Did you see that? When that boy couldn't get their attention and tried too hard, he almost drowned."

"Yeah, so?"

"So? His father obviously came running and showered all his love on him, which is what he wanted a few minutes ago. Maybe you should do something similar," I said.

"Like what? You want me to jump into the river?" she asked.

"I don't know, play your X-factor. Come on! Do something he doesn't expect you to. Make him feel a bit insecure... jealous. You know what I am talking about?"

Finally a little smile appeared on her face. "You are really wicked!" she remarked.

"Hey! He is my best friend. Besides, every person is a hero in his own mind. You just need to wake the hero up in them!" I winked at her. I took it to be a bit harmless, to be honest, just to ignite some passion between them. We walked back to the hotel and decided to freshen up and attend it in the evening.

❖

Haridwar felt like a war zone by twilight. The three of us stood staring at Har ki Pauri ghat with our backpacks. I had my camera in hand. I wanted to capture the aarti up close. However, it was impossible to move, even an inch; there were people everywhere. It seemed as though the entire world had decided to attend the aarti. And then, emailed their friends to attend it too!

For a second, we felt like running back to our hotel when we saw the crowd. The evening aarti, the masses taking a royal dip in the Ganga and the long procession of the holy fire was all too much after a while. Honestly, we were looking for cover after having our foreheads pasted with a tilak for the umpteenth time.

We managed to slip out, but got separated. I had ended up on a relatively secluded corner of the ghats, at least a kilometer away from the main area of action. I decided to buy some bhel puri for dinner. Some distance ahead, I could see the Kumbh Mela and its glitterati with giant-wheels and flashy lights. However, it didn't make sense to escape from a sea of people only to join another mob. I ate my bhel puri in silence and stared at the river.

"Take a dip in the holy river!"

That was the only piece of advice my father gave me when I told him about my decision to take this trip. I stripped down to my boxers and waded into the freaking cold water slowly. I was determined and kept going till I was shoulder-deep in the water. I folded my hands in prayer and kept my eyes closed. That was the supposed thing to do when you try to wash away your sins.

"You know what your problem is? You only care about yourself!" she shouted at me. I listened. "You think it isn't easy for you to adjust with me. Tell you what! It is tougher for me to walk into this new household and get used to your tantrums, besides your father's!"

I kept listening, sitting mutely at the huge dining table.

"And yes, your father, the useless bugger that he is. Couldn't keep his first wife happy. I told him before also that it won't be easy to live with a twenty-year-old son. But what can he understand? I am stuck in this house!" she kept cursing him. All I could do was listen. I didn't choose her. I didn't choose my parents' separation either. When I had to live with it, I guess I had to get used to living with this as well.

My father walked in with two of his employees behind him. The hall turned silent. "What's going on here?" His loud, authoritative voice filled the huge drawing room. His wife (not my mother, mind you) adjusted herself and made a face. He understood and looked at me for answers.

"Nothing, Dad! When you have time, please sign these forms and ask your accountant to make a draft for five lakhs for me." I plonked a set of papers on the dining table and left.

After sucking in the melodrama of my father's household for six months, I decided to move out. Not that he was a bad person. He was so engaged in expanding his already huge business empire that he seldom had any time for me. His new wife, well, my stepmom – she and I didn't click. At some level, it was obvious that she'd be happier if I lived separately or with my own mother. However, I wanted a family, a home, and that's why I came to live with them immediately after my graduation. But barely a few months into that new lifestyle, I realized it wasn't the home I wanted.

My own mother seemed to care very little for me, anyway, and chose to divorce her husband at an age when most people comfortably settle in their lives and with their partners. If she really was unhappy, why did she bear him for eighteen years? Why did she leave him without discussing it with me properly? All I got was a phone call in the first year in the hostel, that something irreparable had happened between them and she was leaving us for good. As a son, as their family, I deserved more participation and definitely proper intimation than a mere phone call!

Although Dad did come to meet me a few times, he never talked about what happened between them. I didn't ask. She simply disappeared from my life and failed as a mother, in my books. Though I knew where she was, I had no reason to look for her after I completed college. But whatever may have happened in the past, this home wasn't reasonable for me.

With a heavy heart, I decided to pursue a Master's program in the suburbs. I was telling my stepmom about it when she broke into this exaggerated-emotional piece. Yeah, she did fake the whole 'new-family' stuff, and she knew nothing about me. Why all this 'seek my permission' crap?

The next morning, my father was standing in my room. He came to my bed and stroked my head lightly, "Abhay, I know we have been very unfair with you. Both me and your mother."

I got up. Fathers and sons rarely have physical intimacy, and we were no different. He continued, "It doesn't mean we don't care for you. However, the way things are, it is difficult for you. I know. That's a regret I guess I have to live with, for life."

I was choked with emotion.

"But I don't want you to suffer for your parents' mistake. Nor do I want you to have any regrets later in life. You are free to attend this course or do anything else you want. It's not that I am not appreciative of your choice, neither is your mother. That's why she was questioning you yesterday. But yes, I want you to live your own life. Don't have regrets later."

For the first time, I felt he was not wrong. I began having pangs of guilt. My real intention was to dupe him into believing that I'd be going to study when in reality I just wanted to move out of his house. But I decided to keep that secret to myself. I nodded in agreement and shook hands with him. It was to mark that we understood each other perfectly, that we probably weren't going to see each other as regularly now. In less than a week, I left home and settled into a studio apartment near my institute in Gurgaon.

My feet were numb because of the cold. That was when I returned to my senses. I had been in the cold water for less than five minutes, but my whole body shivered badly. I walked swiftly towards the shore, and then realized that I did not even have a towel to dry up. Hastily, I wore my clothes and started running towards the road to catch an auto that would take me back. Sneezing continuously in the auto, I hoped that at least the sin of my lie or partial truth to my father had been done away with, thanks to River Ganga.

The litmus test – Leh and Ladakh

The next morning, there was a loud bang on the door that woke me up. "Open up, you idiot!" Sasha was shouting from outside. I got to the gate, rubbing my eyes. Sasha was in his jeans, and looking super upset. He had every reason to. I remembered how I did not bother to check his whereabouts the previous night. I had just crashed in bed when I returned from my holy dip. Worse still, I had bolted the door from inside.

Sasha sat on my bed and started abusing me. I pulled up a stool and sat by him. "Sorry bro. I was too preoccupied with something."

He looked around and his eyes lit up, "Did you get a girl in here?"

"No man, I mean I got emotional thinking about something and then just took a dip in Ganga. It was so cold. I just crashed when I reached."

"Stop lying, you moron! I can see your clothes all over the place. Don't tell me I slept on the floor in Unnati's room for nothing!" he shouted at me.

"That's because they were wet. Hey, you slept on the floor? Why, are you gay?"

He picked up the bedside telephone and threw at me. Luckily, it was wired and before it could hit me, it fell on the floor and broke. "What's wrong with you?"

"Fucker, what did you tell her? That she needs to get my attention? She did not even let me touch her hand, let alone sleep in the same bed. She is a sati-savitri now, I tell you!"

That was it! So Miss Unnati, faking to sound super pleased at my words of wisdom last afternoon, not only chose to dump them but also told her boyfriend all that I said. I picked up the broken pieces of the phone and assembled the phone back and sat next to him. "What did she tell you?"

"That she needs to play up her X-factor to get my attention and some such shit. Man, you should've suggested that she learns how to cook if she really wants to please me!"

"See, that's your problem. You just can't keep food out of your head. That's what she was complaining to me about. I just gave her an advice in general."

"In general? My foot! Anyway, forget it. My back is hurting badly and I'm going to take a nap.

Two hours later, we were standing at the reception to check out. A group of backpackers had just returned from Rishikesh and informed us that the river rafting had to be cancelled because of poor weather. It meant that we had very little reason to make the forty kilometer drive. We decided to skip it, and drive straight to our next destination.

Soon, we were all shouting goodbye from the Little Beast's open windows to Haridwar and its mayhem. In two days, we had experienced the complete silence of the jungle and a virtual stampede of thousands of people.

"Life can flip a hundred and eighty degrees, in a matter of days…"

Blue's *One Love* played loud, echoing my thoughts.

We were now geared up for our first long stint in the car. Technically it was a road trip, but the distance measured over the last couple of days was peanuts to say the least. Our real test to survive the country roads, to endure long hours sitting in that 10x5 space and the exhaustion of a road trip was now going to be tested. Somehow, all three of us were thinking about it, because we all chose to remain silent. We had planned to cover a thousand kilometers from Haridwar to Ladakh in around three days and gave ourselves twelve hours of traveling time each day with stopovers in Manali and Lahaul-Spiti.

Sasha and I had spoken to a couple of veteran travelers and taken their advice. They all had the same thing to say. "Once you reach Ladakh by road, you will virtually be dead. It looks cool to see those boys do it in movies like *3 Idiots* or hear about bikers setting out for the Delhi-Manali route and then onwards on the Manali-Ladakh route on their Enfields. But, you are running a marathon here and not a sprint. You have a long tour to unfold and cannot afford to give up at Ladakh. The weather acclimatization sucks."

We gave them our thumbs-down the moment they left. Our real litmus test had begun. In cricketing terms, we decided to take it like a test match, session-by-session – morning-to-evening driving and then retiring to any roadside hotel available, only to resolute to a better performance the next day. We chose not to have a longer stopover at Manali, which, in hindsight, was a mistake.

As Sasha drove with Unnati next to him, I sat in the backseat and decided to glance through what I had shot so far. The best part of the raw footage was where we struggled the most – standing on the riverbank and capturing the diyas floating and the crowd raising lights. It looked divine. It's funny, coz we hated standing there amidst the crowd. But after editing this clip, it would possibly constitute one of the finest parts of our road-movie!

That's what life is all about. You may hate it one moment, but later on, that very moment may become your most cherished memory.

I saw Sashank staring at me from the rear-view mirror. I stared back. It looked like he was trying to tell me something. He was blinking his eyes swiftly and then half-opened his mouth, expelling air out, gesturing that I should snore. I understood and feigned having gone to sleep. He smiled in the rear-view mirror again and turned to Unnati, "Beautiful weather outside, isn't it sweetheart?" She didn't react. "Ah, I just wish we had a tea stall nearby where we can sit, hand-in-hand, sipping tea, occasionally dipping Parle-G biscuits into the tea," he said and sighed.

She was in no mood to speak. I laughed inside my head. My friend juxtaposed romance and food beautifully.

He moved his left hand and rubbed her shoulder lightly. After a minute or so, Unnati eased and started craning her neck in all directions. I could sense the heat between them rise slowly. Soon her neck bent sideways and rested on his hand, meaning that my friend had only one hand left to navigate the car.

"Baby, I miss having some alone time with you," Unnati said in a low voice.

Great, I thought. So she wants my bromance with Sashank to pave way for their 'alone' time. I suddenly felt unwanted in my own car!

"I know that, coochie-pie. But this is fun too. We are alone for the next three months, imagine!"

"Yes, but you don't give me your attention at all, the way you used to, earlier. Remember our college days? You used to do the silliest of things for me, to make me happy." She sighed, rubbing her neck against his arm.

Sasha knew that I could hear their conversation and was visibly embarrassed. He had the difficult task of changing the topic and not letting his girl down. Otherwise, she was likely to speak about more personal stuff. It's funny, men like to brag about being macho all the time, but never share their sensitive side with each other.

"I promise you, sweetie, I will take you out at least ten times throughout this trip too, and ask Abhay to stay out of it," he said lovingly and then he kissed her forehead. She made a sound that meant approval. Sasha leaned further into her, doing things that I shouldn't be mentioning.

Suddenly, there was a loud thud. We hit a huge speed-breaker, which these lovers obviously didn't notice. Our car's chassis kissed the rough road beneath and the screeching sound meant that there was obvious damage. The car veered for a second when Sasha applied the brakes suddenly to regain control. But it ended up hitting a roadside pavement lightly. I woke up and saw them with their mouths wide open, and in a state of a shock. I immediately got down to do a post-mortem. Apart from a few scratches on the front bumper, there were no obvious damages.

Sasha got off too.

"Are you done?"

"What?" he didn't get the sarcasm.

I repeated, "Are you done with spitting into her, or should we wait for a truck to hit us?" I hissed.

He pushed me. "What's wrong with you man? It was an accident!"

We argued while Miss Coochie Pie kept sitting in her seat, probably out of guilt. Even during the argument, I couldn't stop thinking about her. She was my best buddy's girlfriend and someone with a sweet voice till a few days ago. Now she seemed so incomprehensible.

We decided that I was going to drive for the next three months. We both knew it wasn't practical, but we still had to agree upon it at least for that moment. Getting into the driver's seat, I told her, "You can sit in the back if you want to. I don't mind sitting alone." Unnati gawked at Sasha in terror and settled back into her seat.

I had clearly spoiled their moment, but our safety and trip were more important. I felt like their parent again and decided to put on earphones and listen to music for the rest of the day. Since there was no further action, we kept driving, stopping only for a quick lunch break at a highway shack near Baddi. We drove on until the evening. Though the roads weren't exactly smooth, by 7:00 we finally reached the outskirts of Manali. I patted myself mentally for covering such a vast distance by myself. For the first time, I felt the fatigue of driving and got a feel of how much driving we had in store for us.

That night, we checked in at a hotel called Moonlight. But the only tryst with moonlight we had was from our rooms – which were right on the roof.

Early next morning, the drive began to take a toll on me. It was through a hilly area, as we were now climbing the Rohtang Pass. It had opened only a couple of days ago. Secondly, the bed I had slept in the previous night hadn't been comfortable. After much resistance, I handed over Little Beast's wheels to Sasha, though this time I decided to sit next to him, thereby killing all possibilities.

By early afternoon, we were approaching Keylong and it started getting colder. We had our first brush with the extreme temperature and altitude as we stopped near a hill for a shoot. We parked our now dusty and frozen car at Tashi Delek, a family restaurant in Keylong village, whose momos are always a hit back home in Dilli Haat. We got a chance to speak to some locals and fellow travelers. Noticing a young gora backpacker, we decided to join him to share insights. Gorging on pork and chicken momos, we discussed our plan to not stay at Jispa or even Darcha and halt at Sarchu, barely 300 kilometers from Ladakh. He got excited and asked if he could join us.

"Are you sure? You have white skin. It needs more time to adjust in our Indian conditions after all," I joked.

"Don't worry, mate. The muscles underneath aren't easy to break. I love your idea of this road trip. Tell you what, when I get back to Portugal, I will convince my buddies to take a similar trip across Europe. Maybe you can take your road movie international, Abhay, and feature us in your European chapter!" Emmanuel said. Pointing at Unnati, he added, "Though it will be difficult to find a voice as beautiful as hers!"

Unnati beamed. Emmanuel had scored and the lady's approval meant we had a companion for the rest of our day's journey. We wrapped up lunch and redirected our car towards the mountain range, taking a fellow tourist and some momos along. During the journey, Emmanuel shared his own travel experiences, which included things as adventurous as scuba diving in the Australian Great Barrier Reef and as adrenalin pumping as going to watch the football world cup in Brazil with no money in his pocket! Listening to him helped us cope with those brazen, bumpy roads.

Finally, we retired at Sarchu. It was pitch dark when we reached. It looked like an aloof region till we reached a checkpost that signaled that we were at the Himachal Pradesh border and about to enter Ladakh.

We bid goodbye to Emmanuel at this point, as he had to follow the long procedural formalities for foreigners when they entered the region. A policeman guarding the post came up to us in surprise and said, "I have never seen anyone drive this late into this area. You guys should have stopped much earlier. One can catch a cold easily!" he said, snapping his fingers. We got off and looked at each other. Thankfully, we looked alive, though we did feel a bit of mountain sickness. We decided to swallow a pill each and spend the night inside a makeshift military camp without further ado.

"You want me to be successful? Is that why you left me? Is that all you have to say, Mummy?" I asked her furiously on the phone. It was only her second phone call since she gave me the news of her separation.

"Abhay, you don't understand. Your father loves you too. Besides, he is rich. What could I have offered you?" she sobbed.

"So it's about money, right? He has more money, so he gets to keep me. Am I agarment at Gucci that I can be taken by whoever has more moolah? What about me? What if I want to live with the both of you or neither at all?" I asked.

"Calm down, Abhay. I have lived with him for eighteen years. You have no idea how I prayed for this time to pass, taking care of the responsibilities and the family for the sake of society. I thought when my son would be old enough to understand it, I could take this step and live a life of my own and chase passions that I couldn't otherwise fulfill!" She was crying.

I waited for her sobs to mellow down. I then gave her a piece of my mind. "So it's my fault, right? If you really were waiting for me to grow up all these years, while making a sacrifice, couldn't you make me a part of your decision? How would I cope with all these years of loneliness to come? How would I deal with the tag of 'divorced parents' for the rest of my life? How would I tell my future wife that I could take care of her? Won't she question my stained blood and my virtues?"

She sobbed even more and replied sarcastically, "Very nice, beta! This is a good reward for bringing you up. This is the 'modern era' after all. One shouldn't expect anything from their children these days!"

I don't know what else she expected from this conversation. She just kept crying, perhaps hoping that her suffering would make me feel any better. I decided to hang up. Why do parents feel they have a right to do anything or leave their children in any situation, and then blame 'modern' society? I can never accept their separation. I mean, imagine living with two people, a man and a woman for all your life, and then suddenly being told one day that it was all a lie, that they were living it this way for your sake? It's worse than living with just one of them right from the start. Even if they were to separate, I expected her to meet me, discuss possibilities and repercussions of their decisions with me, and then let me choose if I supported her or not. She owed me a huge apology for doing all this to me.

❖

I woke up drenched in sweat. My wristwatch showed 5:00 AM. It was still dark outside. The place was at its coldest at that hour. My mental turbulence, however, beat all external conditions. Or maybe it was the pill.

I decided not to wake the other two. I walked outside, picking up my muffler as I went out. The sun was slowly rising, throwing a hint of its bright rays from the Himalayan mountain range staring from the other end.

I noticed two huge trees standing on opposite sides of the road in front. Strangely, one was tall and strong, but bare. The other was very small, but full of green leaves. The empty branches on the first one cut a sorry figure. I wondered how the Almighty didn't bless this huge tree equally, especially as it grew so close to the other one. Sasha came out of the tent, rubbing his eyes. I looked at him and immediately thought of him as the green tree while I was the haggard one.

Yes, he was my best friend, my non-biological brother. But for a second, I was jealous of him. He had a huge family; his parents lived together, his uncles, his elder brothers and their wives included. Now, he had a girlfriend too, who would soon be a part of the family, while I would live all alone and have my so-called parents living somewhere else.

"Are you alright, Abhay?" chucked Unnati from the backseat. I was driving again. We started early in the morning to try and reach Leh by the evening. It was a far-fetched thought, to say the least.

The dream this morning had a longer hangover than expected. Despite the beautiful landscapes on both sides, I wasn't my usual self. "Yes, I am fine," I said, and added curtly, "If I wasn't, I'd tell you. I am sure it will be broadcast well then."

She knew what I was talking about. Sasha was groggy and therefore lay like an abandoned potato sack.

"Are you upset with me because I told him about the ideas you gave me?"

"Shouldn't I be?"

"No. On the contrary, your suggestions did work! I made him jealous and crave for me, albeit in my own way. But the basic thought was yours."

Just then, Sashank farted loudly. He didn't care though, and slept more soundly. We both laughed, looking at each other in the rear-view mirror.

"Maybe. What exactly did you do to make him jealous?"

"You said to play the girl card. I did. My style was my own, though. I dressed and looked my best for him, but asked him to back off at the same time!" She smiled viciously. Now I knew why Sasha had to sleep on the floor.

"And then you told him everything..."

"Not fair, Abhay! No, I didn't tell him that you told me to make him jealous and insecure. I didn't tell him that. I just said Ab suggested that I attract your attention and that's why I am dressed up for you. Is that a bad way of saying it? You wanted him to value me more, one way or the other, right?"

She was right. Suddenly the entire perspective of looking at it changed. She sat back. I became relaxed and poured my heart to her. "You know, sometimes I feel he is so lucky. He has a family to back him up, a crisp live-to-eat attitude and a loyal girlfriend like you. I look like such a loser, living alone and nobody but a few friends to share my heart with."

"Well, it's because you don't have a woman to confide in. I know you're not on talking terms with your mother. Believe me, we are best at handling emotions. You just have a useless bunch of male friends!" she replied acting like a grandmother.

"Did you realize you just called your boyfriend useless?"

"I know. That he is. Anyway, it's not about him. Tell me, what you were saying?"

"Well, to start with, I have hated living alone. People may think of it as very cool, but it's really not. Imagine getting up every morning and eating your breakfast alone. Or returning home every night and not saying goodnight to anybody. You guys have family back home and can never understand that feeling..."

She was a good listener and nodded, encouraging me to continue. "I can't come to terms with my parents' separation. They moved on with their choices and I ended up being a victim of their mistakes." Just to lighten myself up, I added, "Chuck it, talk about something else!"

"Talking about relationships, well, I am not too well placed either. I want marriage sooner than later now. I am at that age, but he doesn't seem ready or care about it," she quipped. Before I could react, she added, "But hey, I don't lose hope. And you shouldn't too. Your past cannot be changed, but trust your destiny to have someone special hidden for you – who can talk to you, share her soul with you and bring you breakfast in bed."

"At least you have found that special person," I remarked.

Her face tightened. No words were exchanged. Sasha's second fart broke the silence and he got up slowly, putting our topical conversation on hold.

He yawned and said, "I am hungry, let's stop somewhere!"

"Your morning poori-aloo is still smelling. And you are hungry again?" I mock yelled.

"Yeah bhai, very!" he said rubbing his tummy. I groaned. Luckily, there were no roadside eateries for miles, and all he could do was complain and sulk. When we stopped, he ate like a famine-struck soul of Sudan and fortunately allowed me to drive peacefully after that.

The next few hours were spent driving. I would easily rank that as the most taxing drive of the entire trip, even though, every now and then, we did stop to admire the beauty all around us. Finally, on day four of our drive from Haridwar, we arrived at Leh in the afternoon.

As we stepped out of our dusty EcoSport near the U-shaped traffic signboard that read 'Welcome to Leh,' I expected more enthusiasm from all of us. This was to be the crowning glory of our trip – the most revered destination of our lives. Maybe it was the rigorous three-and-a-half days of driving. Maybe it was the extreme temperature in the region. Or maybe my own emotional state. I really didn't know. But, I could see fatigue even on my friends' faces as they quietly posed with 'No.4' placards and raised hands.

Instead of staying at a hotel, we chose to stay at a guesthouse-styled accommodation with a family. Sasha's uncle recommended a middle-aged couple who had converted their bungalow into a guesthouse, catering only to young travellers.

Diki and Dorjee, the inhabitants of the Hidden Lake Guesthouse, were affable and welcoming. Both were locals. Dorjee worked for a fat pay cheque in a remote corner of Europe before he realized, one winter, that the alienating isolation was getting the better of him. He returned to his native land, and bought this property with his savings. Diki, his better half, was a superb cook and had a penchant for meeting new people. Together, they converted their huge home into an affordable and warm place to stay for adventure junkies. One look at them, and you visualize how you want your old age to be.

For the next few days, they took such good care of us that Ladakh held the best memories from our trip. Even though they were not required to, they became our unpaid tour guides and accompanied us to all common and hidden breathtaking sights in and around their domain – Leh Palace, Pangong River, the sanctuaries, muesuems, gompas, and stupas. Dorjee took us on a short trek from Spituk Matho, which was mainly through barren land, but offered jaw dropping views of the mountain ranges.

"It is so beautiful!" Unnati remarked as we stopped for a breather beside a monastery. It was a huge white structure against an otherwise brownish-greenish mountain range. I removed my Oakley and sat on a rock, capturing the view. Sashank and Dorjee sat down on the pavement for rest. For someone of Sasha's girth, I admired his stamina to walk.

"So tell me Dorjee, are non-Tibetan couples allowed to get married at these monasteries?" she winked at him as she asked this question.

Dorjee played along. "Yeah sure, why not? Do you want me to talk to them? We can organize one for you in an hour or so."

Sashank's mouth fell half-open, and for the first time ever, it was not for the lack of food. He looked at me. I said, "Well, if you two are okay, who am I to complain? I will send a postcard home. Don't worry about them buddy, they will be happy for you!"

He stammered, "B... baby...but...you...you always wanted a fancy wedding..." he was still looking like a dead duck.

"Don't worry, my boy. Weddings in our region can be as grand as you want them to be. We will invite the whole village and there will be dancing all evening. We will treat all guests with specially sourced single-malt scotch," Dorjee said.

Sasha gave him a glare that seemed to say, 'I will pay you double the rent, but please don't ignite further ideas!'

After what appeared to be more than a minute, Unnati burst laughing. Dorjee and I laughed along, as Sasha kept staring at us in confusion. I informed him, "Dude, it's where monks and nuns live. Remember nuns? Those women who denounce worldly pleasures for spiritual conquests or whatever? They won't make it a wedding pandal even if it were the last building standing!"

Now it was his turn to smile in embarrassment. "I knew it all along."

After a good laugh, we decided to go back to the guest house.

Just then, Unnati fell down. Dorjee and I ran to her. She lay motionless. Dorjee quickly uncorked his bottle of water and splashed a few droplets on her face. He lightly rubbed her head and palm together as she slowly came back to her senses, complaining of a terrible headache. As she got up, she felt something building in her stomach.She quickly ran to a corner and puked. I looked at

Sasha for answers. He had none. He went to her, and caressing her back, asked softly, "Are you okay, Unns?"

"I feel sick!" she murmured. "Please leave me alone," she said, pushing his hand aside and resting on the ground.

I ran to them and took Sashank to a corner, shouting at him. "You bastard, don't you have any patience, what the hell did you do to her?"

He took a minute before understanding me. "Oh, no no. It's... it's not that, bhai. You are getting it all wrong!"

"You were all over her in the car. Do you think I am blind? Maybe we should get you two married after all!"

"Relax boys," interrupted Dorjee. "It's high Altitude Mountain Sickness (AMS) that she is experiencing here. If anything, she should be fine in a day or two. I have medication back in the village."

"What the fuck is that?" Unnati asked, still on the ground.

"Well, when you can't acclimatize properly to high altitude, you tend to have nausea and severe headaches. It's mild, though. I am sure you got injected for the same before arriving here."

We looked at each other. Dorjee understood. "Folly, rather the impatience of youth. Well, don't worry, let's just go back and I will take care of it."

Unnati couldn't get up at all. We made a makeshift stretcher after borrowing a broken bed and a quilt from the kind monks and trekked back to the guesthouse. Under expert guidance of Dorjee and the motherly care of Diki, Unnati was much better in a couple of days. Dorjee assured us that she would get over it quickly too, and was otherwise good to resume the tour. We had another long drive ahead of us, and we had already extended our stay in Ladakh. But now, it was time to bid goodbye.

Letting down
Bhagat Singh

Anyone planning a long drive back from Ladakh can be given one piece of advice – Don't do it! It is mentally and physically draining to be in Leh, and then to drive down. Driving by yourself should be a big no-no on any sane person's list.

But as Dorjee said 'we were insane to the point of evoking jealousy in him', he bid us goodbye. More so, he warned that we were going to travel with a girl who had barely recovered from AMS and that we had chosen to travel via NH-1, or the Srinagar-Leh Highway, which passed through Kargil.

"Usually, people do it the other way around. They come through this route so they can gradually acclimatize with high altitude and return via Manali. You guys are bonkers!" he remarked, giving us some footage for my film. We waved goodbye to Diki. She returned a smile, wiping her eyes. I wondered if she cried after every guest left, or if we were really that special. I also wondered why such a lovely couple didn't have kids of their own.

With those thoughts in mind, Sasha drove us early in the morning to the higher mountain peaks, which I hoped we would cross to reach Srinagar by the night. By late afternoon, we had driven for seven hours straight, and were approaching Kargil. We stopped at the visitor's check-post to register ourselves. The area had come into prominence after the 1999 war. There were over a hundred tourists lined up. Most were college students or younger. I prepared my camera to shoot a video of all of them. They all seemed to validate the fact that the offbeat yet relevant Kargil-Drass conjured more patriotism than a visit to the Wagah Border. Buoyed by their enthusiasm, we decided to skip lunch and visit the Drass War Memorial and Tiger Hill viewpoint first. For once, even Sashank didn't mind. I had never experienced goose bumps the way I did when we stopped at the War Memorial. The place totally floors you. You can see Indian flags, read stories of heroes from the Indian Army who had fought in the battle, read their names – and it all grows on you within a few minutes.

We left Kargil after a hearty meal at the Army Canteen beside the memorial. The main hurdle for the 140 kilometer drive to Srinagar was that we had to navigate through the Zoji La Pass, which is almost always covered with snow. I felt sorry for my car as we drove on this stretch. I decided to visit a good garage in Srinagar the next day for a quick check.

We were to halt in Srinagar for the night, and then start driving the next day, rather early on in the morning. We felt like zombies after having spent over a hundred hours on the road in the last ten days. Unnati argued that she was not up to facing the camera any further till she had a chance to visit a parlor. We decided on a longer halt once we entered Punjab. As we breezed past Vijaypur, a state-border town of Jammu and Kashmir, we bid goodbye to the mountains. The Punjabi grasslands began appearing on both sides of the road. Unnati's genes started having their effect. Her reticence since fainting that day disappeared quickly as she starting jumping in her seat.

"What?" I questioned her loudly.

"Please stop the car. I need to pee badly!" she shouted back.

I parked on the side of the road, and Unnati and Sasha got off to look for a place. It was the fourth or fifth stop since our journey had begun and she was doing her bit to contribute to our beloved Prime Minister's 'Swachh Bharat' campaign.

We grabbed a quick bite at Pathankot – a super calorie-rich Punjabi meal. After his second glass of lassi, Sashank reminded us not to eat too much as he wanted to reach Amritsar's Bharawan-da-dhaba, a popular small-scale eatery, on an empty stomach. I abused my car, kicking it into speed at full throttle. We sustained bumpy roads to be able to drive at full speed and reached Amritsar by late evening. A late night visit to a well-lit and decorated Golden Temple made our fatigue vanish.

The next morning's visit to Wagah Border deserves a dedicated chapter in itself. We had sworn to each other that we wouldn't do it, but both Sasha and I had smuggled our Indian cricket team's jerseys. To each other's surprise, we both wore it in the morning. Unnati was also in blue, and cursed us immediately when she saw us stepping out of our room, "Not cool guys. How old are you? Sixteen?"

Sasha grinned. "He broke the pact!" We had both decided not to 'follow the herd' and wear our team India t-shirts to the Wagah Border. It was what most young people did. The temptation was just too strong.

"Whatever! Let's just go."

Instead of driving from our hotel to the border, we hired a local jeep, a common mode of conveyance in the area. The jeep driver promised us good seats. Even though the flag ceremony began mid-afternoon, we reached early at noon, and grabbed snacks before entering the main area.

"Last morning at Kargil, and now at Wagah. I have gone so far from myself!" I realized as I entered through a huge security point to witness a sea of people. Though the previous day was more about respect for our motherland and was a pure feeling, that day seemed like a cricket match. Everyone on this side of the border was shouting 'India India' at the peak of their voices, and the atmosphere was punctuated by the sound of trumpets. Caps with the word 'India' painted on, flags, t-shirts and even the odd umbrella with our tricolor painted on it were seen all around.

Then, Unnati whispered in my ear, "What's the point of shouting in favor of India when there is no opposition? The Pakistanis can't hear us, can they?" I laughed out aloud but hushed her, lest someone may hear her and throw us out.

A huge wall separated the main seating area and two gates were perpendicular to each other, facing huge lines of people. There were alert security guards on both sides, frisking entrants almost to the point of molestation. Movement was thus as slow as it could be. With nothing else to do but to wait patiently, I tried a friendly chat with a person behind me. "Is this your first time here?"

He didn't reply. I smiled to check if he had heard me or not. In response, he shifted his gaze ahead, twitched a finger up his nose and folded his arms.

"Weirdo!" Sasha said.

We both looked ahead and engaged in our own banter.

"Unfortunately, we won't be able to shoot once we are in the main area. So let's just try and shoot some footage here!" I told my friends who nodded.

"Did you say shoot?" the man behind me asked me, sounding worried. I was glad he responded. There was at least something that shook him enough to part those lips.

"Yes, oh sorry I didn't know you heard me. Very sorry! Please. Continue!" I looked at him and turned around, winking at Sasha. He was a bit flustered.

He said, "Huh! Do you think I am a fool? Go do this time-pass somewhere else."

Playing along, Unnati moved closer to him and me and said, "Shhh shh if anyone hears you, I swear I will open it right here!" He stared at her, bewildered. Like me, he also seemed to feel that she was too cute to be a bad woman. But then Sasha joined in, and that gave him second thoughts.

"Boss, what the hell is going on? Who is he, and why is he talking to us? Let's just focus on our job and... and... ask him to fuck off!"

The man was sure that there was something fishy going on. He moved away from the queue and began walking swiftly in the other direction. We laughed. He was probably going to stand in the other line. Worse still, he'd be looking for an auto and head back to his hotel.

The queue, for some reason, was moving too slowly. We were getting impatient. Suddenly, a voice over the hooter announced, "Kindly be seated or remain wherever you are. Nobody is allowed to enter through the main gate or exit this compound for the next sixty minutes. We will make the next announcement very shortly."

"What the hell?"

"It's so hot. At least let us in!" someone shouted.

"There must be some super VVIP coming, that's why we commoners are forced to wait here!" someone else cried. Everyone laughed.

We waited anxiously to see what was going on. There was some movement behind us. I saw a group of police officers and a few other people moving from a distance, checking everyone in our queue. However, my eyes widened when I saw him – the guy behind us! The faint-hearted wimp! He hadn't run away or joined another queue, but had gone to the security personnel! He had blown our prank out of proportion. This hold up in the queue was because of us, and now, the policemen were approaching us fast.

My heart stopped. I kicked Sasha who was exchanging silly nothings with Unnati.I pointed at the men. Both of them froze, and stood with their mouths open. Unnati regained her composure and said, "Guys we will tell them that it was a joke. This guy took it too seriously!"

"Why would they believe us? They will interrogate us if we don't divulge our 'plan,'" I told them wisely.

To date, I don't know if I was correct or not.

"So what do we do?"

"Let's just split. Maybe he won't recognize us. Even if he does, we will tell the police that he must have had bhang or something as each of us is alone here," Sasha said.

"Good idea. Unnati, look ahead at those guys. I am sure they won't mind you breaking the line. Sasha, move to the queue on the right. I will stay here," I said. Meanwhile, the man with the head of security had moved closer.

We started following our plan. As Sasha moved from the queue, and was in the middle of both the queues, the man pointed at him and shouted, "That's him! There he is!" Everyone started looking in Sasha's direction. I realized the folly of our plan. Sasha was too big to miss. I should have changed lines instead.

He stood there, dumbfounded, as though he had been caught cheating in an exam. In a quick motion, I saw the security chief loosen his tie and drop his walkie-talkie to start running towards Sasha. His team followed him. We had to do something quickly. It was my territory. I looked at my friends staring at me for answers. I lowered my head and shouted at the peak of my voice, "Bomb, oh no, there is a bomb here!" and started running.

In the next second, there was utter chaos as people ran helter skelter. Though the compound's entry points were sealed with barricades, within a few minutes the crowd was on the other side, running in all directions. I just kept running as fast as I could. Looking behind, I saw mayhem and mentally cursed myself for causing it. I finally stopped for a breather near an ice cream vendor, a good distance away from the spot. People had scattered everywhere, but thankfully, Unnati kept her cool and had followed me. She stopped right next to me. Catching her breath, she asked, "Good thinking AB! Where's Sasha?"

I offered her some water, "You think I have a clue?"

"What? You didn't follow him? Or even ask him to come along? What if he had gotten caught? After all, every security man there was looking at him! They will even question him for this bomb now. Oh no no no!" She was hysterical.

"Relax. I know him. He wouldn't have wasted a minute in running away." I doubted myself as I said this.

"Let's go back and look for him."

"Are you mad? If they catch us, we are certainly going to jail!"

"And what if Sasha is already in jail by now?" She was indeed getting mad.

"No way can they catch him! There were at least five thousand people there, maybe more! They'd be busier restoring everything than catching him," I said.

She didn't bother letting me finish my line. She had already started walking in the other direction. After a few seconds or so, I jogged and reached her. I said, "You are right. If he is caught, we must suffer too. We were in this together after all!"

She turned to me and said, "Do you have any idea of the ramifications of this? Even if they check us thoroughly, and are convinced that we are innocent, they will still punish us for causing this bomb scare. What if people were injured in all this?"

She was right. But I still said, "I don't know all that. I just knew that I had to help my friend escape at any cost!" We walked silently and slowly. We saw people all over the road, running in all directions. There were some army men too, trying to get the traffic in order.

I heard someone calling my name, and it sounded like Sasha. We stopped and turned to look. He was shouting from the window of our hired taxi.

"Our car!" Unnati shouted and ran towards it as I followed. It was in the middle of a packed street filled with cars. Each vehicle honked loudly, and we didn't waste time in getting in. We rolled up the windows instantly. I have never been more relieved to see his massive face as I was then. All the three of us fit into the backseat and shared a hug. Our driver shouted at somebody on the road to move quickly. He turned to us and I asked him, "What happened here, paaji?"

His reply broke my heart, "Nothing sir, some miscreants caused a bomb scare. I doubt they really had one. Otherwise they'd have blown it up by now. Stupid people don't have any idea of the impact of such things. This area is probably going to be closed for some time, I guess. This will cause a massive loss of business for us, not to forget the face-down that our military has to bear, in front of the others across the border!"

No words were exchanged. It was too difficult to accept or talk about the culprits, who, as it turned out, had been drenched in national spirit the previous day, and had just caused massive embarrassment at another post on our country's international boundary. We endured the painful journey back to Amritsar, and our hotel.

When we reached the hotel, Sashank broke the silence. "I don't think we should be staying in Amritsar for too long. There may be policemen checking the hotels and the main exit points soon." He was right.

On the flipside, maybe our fears were misplaced. I mean, what were the chances that the only eyewitness would be standing at every check-post on various roads, railway stations and airports to recognize the culprits? We were no Bhagat Singh or Raj Guru after all – we were just a bunch of idiots. But of course, it isn't wise to take any risk and so, by late afternoon, we were already driving on NH-71 to our next destination – Alwar.

A spooky night

For a while, it felt like I was all alone on this trip. I mean, I had two people but they were no more than mannequins. One had a pretty voice to qualify for this trip. The other was a good sidekick, which justified his presence. But me, the self-perceived hero, the producer of this film, the mastermind of this road-trip, the messiah for the two love-birds – I was the actual fool, not worthy of being here at all. It was my idea to stretch the joke, and it was my idea to cause the fake bomb scare. Unnati was right, even if we were caught for calling the word 'shoot' twice, it wouldn't have meant anything in the bigger scheme of things. The havoc caused later was unpardonable.

Not only were we forced to run away from Amritsar like thieves, but were also responsible for the chaos that probably resulted in injuries to innocent people. Worse, we had no clue now what had happened. We could only wait to catch it in the news later. I jammed the emergency brakes and parked the car in a hurry.

"What the f…?" Sashank shouted as he saw me getting off.

I walked to a shack. I didn't wait for him and just went to the guy behind the counter. The owner was resting his feet on a table, lazing around under a creaking fan. A small television sat before him.

"Big brother, please put on the television. I want to watch the news," I pleaded with him.

"Huh?" he was shocked to see me. His reaction was worrying. It was as though he was about to dismiss me. I added just in time, "Three cups of tea and some biscuits too." That woke him up. He gave me the remote, and made his way to get the tea ready. I switched on the television and flipped to a regional news channel. I expected it to show news of Wagah, since we were barely 50 kilometers from Amritsar. Unnati and Sasha had also joined me by then. Our hearts skipped a beat. We saw a scantily dressed newsreader describing the incident in an extremely high pitch and a worried tone. It sounded like it had made headlines. We sank further in our guilt.

She concluded saying, "Luckily, there were no casualties. Except for a few minor injuries, no other damages have been reported so far. The chief of BSF at Wagah has hinted at possibilities of a false alarm even though investigations are still on."

Unnati sighed while I was full of guilt. We quickly gulped down our tea and got behind the wheel.

My friends may have had made peace with it, but I still couldn't stop thinking. I kept driving in silence without stopping. It was dark by now, but we were still far from Alwar since we hadn't stuck to the plans of starting out in the morning.

On the way, Sasha said, "I don't think we can reach Alwar before midnight. Let us stop over somewhere and spend the night."

"No, we are not stopping anywhere. The roads are not steep anymore. The Little Beast is in good shape," I said.

Sasha still said, "Let me at least eat dinner somewhere. I don't want to wait for Alwar to eat; it's a ghostly town!" he settled back in his seat.

Ghostly town! Yes!

Alwar's Bhangarh Fort is notorious as one of the spookiest places in India. It was supposedly the darling of dare devil souls of all ages. We all grew up hearing stories about the place and wanted to visit it for a very long time. Though people are not allowed to enter the fort after evening hours, the rule was often abused by groups of youngsters who sneaked in with their liquor bottles. Unnati wasn't too keen on including it in the itinerary. She opted to stay at a hotel in town, while we would spend the night at the fort, or do whatever we wanted to. But we kept insisting and Sasha even promised her 'something special' if she joined us.

We never expected to reach Alwar so late though. We raced past the Sariska Wildlife Sanctuary. I checked our calculations, and we hoped to reach it around 11:00. I warned my friends not to have conversations with locals that we were likely to bump into. Google suggested that the locals didn't appreciate trespassing, since they felt that the so-called curse on their town would worsen.

However, with so much darkness and barely lit roads, it was impossible to reach Bhangarh Fort without help. It was pitch-black and a narrow road that had no other traveller except for us. Even if we were to stop to ask for directions, there was no one to help. I finally saw a thin person cycling at a slow speed. He looked like a watchman in his khaki outfit. I stopped the car excitedly, blocking his way. He seemed scared. I opened the door and stepped down to ask him where the fort was. His eyes widened.

"It is around 3 kilometers from here. You cannot get entry now. It is prohibited to enter after sunset. Find shelter in the village and come back tomorrow morning!"

But before he could move, I blocked his way. "Don't say that. We are coming from very far. Please just tell us the route."

He refused. After much prodding, he agreed and then added, "Son, I work as the security guard at the fort. I can tell you that there is no paranormal or ghostly presence there. All this is the villagers' bullshit. But, there is the Aravali Range behind and the Sariska Reserve on the other side. There are wild animals that come for shelter and water, especially at night. It is dangerous to even enter at this hour, let alone stay there."

"No no, we will just see it from outside and come back!" I said.

"As I said, I have been working there for over twenty years. I know that all young people come there for adventure and some adrenalin rush. But believe me, most of them return with nightmares for life!"

Thankfully, Unnati was inside the car and couldn't hear this conversation. I was under my spell. I paid no attention to his warning. I cajoled him instead. "Dada, you take us there, then. We just want to take a round there and will come back peacefully, I swear."

His look suggested that he was not going to take the risk. I offered him money.

"No money is enough to let your remaining days sink into depression! I know a man who went there in his youth. Today, in his forties, he is half-mad and doesn't step out of his home once it is dark outside. Do you think I will go there for some useless piece of paper?"

I was shaken hearing his response. For a man of his means, and the fact that he worked there every day for long hours, I thought he would agree easily. I persisted. "At least keep 500 rupees and drop us there. Otherwise, we may not reach at all!" I handed him a note. He smiled and turned around.

I got into the car and told them that he was going to take us to the fort.

Unnati asked, "But did you ask him if it's safe to go now or not?"

Sasha said, "Come on, Unns! The guy looks like a local and has agreed to take us there and it's almost midnight. It means this is common here. Good call, Ab! Let's go!" He sat back with a smile. I stayed quiet.

Of course, we drove slowly to match his speed, as we encountered a stony road. Honestly, it felt so eerie outside, that for a second, I shared Unnati's fears. After a while, we took a steep turn and saw a huge, rusted iron gate at a little distance.

This was probably the first gate that we had to enter, although vehicles couldn't go beyond this point. We parked our car and stepped out. The man cycled away, but not without giving us a piece of his mind.

"Here you go, boys! I am not a policeman, as otherwise I would have fined you for breaking the rules. My duty hours are over. Otherwise, I'd not have allowed you to enter at all. Whether it is for your good or not, only time will tell. My advice is to go back and come again tomorrow morning. I will take you around this beautiful fort myself. Otherwise, just add yourself to the long list of miseries attached to its curse."

As he sped off, I raised my middle finger.

Unnati wasn't impressed. "Guys, it's a bad idea. What did he mean that it was not his duty hours or else he'd have not allowed us?"

I had to tell her that he worked as a guard at the fort.

"Exactly what is a guard's duty here? It is free entry right, then why do they even require a guard?"

"To ensure that miscreants like us don't break rules and enter past visit hours!" said Sasha as he quickly collected a couple of torches, Swiss-knives, some chips and most importantly, a full bottle of rum, and put them into a bag. Getting past the main gate was easy despite it being locked. Once inside, however, the sound of silence made us freeze. Sasha looked the most confident, while his girl was sweating.

"Bhai, let's sit here for a while. What do you say?" I pointed at a broken wall. They agreed, confirming in my mind that everyone was equally scared. As we leaned back against the wall, Unnati suggested that we take a selfie with card six here. We sat up and huddled with our back to the fort to click it without the camera flash in night mode, and fake smiles. We took the picture. Unnati heaved a deep, urgent sigh on checking the picture in the small screen of her SLR.

"What happened?" asked Sasha.

"Look at this!" she pushed its screen to our faces. Honestly, there was nothing to see. It was a dark picture, even with night vision. "I can't see anything!" I told her.

She sounded scared and half-shouted, "Look at that grey thing behind!" On a closer look, there was some grey haziness, probably a cloud or something. Nothing scandalous.

"I am telling you there is something strange here. Let's go back!" she touched my shoulders saying this.

"Relax Unnati, here have this!" Sasha had miraculously prepared three glasses of drinks and offered her one.

"You fucker, you should have diluted it!" I yelled as I gulped mine, realizing that it was neat. Unnati coughed and choked a little.

"Are you kidding me? I had to pack light. Eat some chips and let me make another round!" he said.

Slowly, we got comfortable with the idea of sitting in a deserted and haunted place in the middle of the night, a place where the faint-hearted barely made it even when the sun shone. Considering that Unnati was one, it made our feat all the more credible.

After half-an-hour or so, we dumped enough rum into our systems to breach the line between sane and crazy. We got onto our feet to make a move. I needed the torch to move ahead. To add to it, the sound of the night – neither completely silent nor noisy, and filled with the buzz of insects – the eeriness of forest and the spookiness of a dilapidated fort, it all gave me goose bumps with every step we took.

We had moved about a hundred meters and were now at the main entrance. It was now that those sounds started becoming stranger.

Suddenly, there was a loud howl, probably from an owl or a flying bat. Unnati gripped my hand tightly. She was between us. I held my video camera and Sasha shone the torch light. Panic had finally struck him, as he squealed, "Mumma..." instinctively. In my heart, I wanted to laugh, but the situation stopped me from doing so. We took baby steps and went inside, and to ease ourselves started talking to each other.

"You know my favorite song?" I asked.

Unnati started singing in reply, *"Tujhe dekha to yeh jaana sanam..."*

"You haven't even seen me yet!" a female voice announced.

We became silent. If there was any uncertainty about the presence of ghosts at Bhangarh Fort, it was immediately dispelled. Someone had answered Unnati, and I was sure that all three of us had heard it. It was so dark that it was impossible to stare at my friends for their reactions, but I thought I had peed in my pants. I was that scared!

Unnati tugged at me to move ahead. It took me a second to realize that I was imagining things, and that she was continuing to sing and walk ahead. Sasha hushed her and shone his torchlight on a big tree in the courtyard. It was huge and shockingly green, contrary to the rest of our surroundings. Its branches were moving swiftly. Suddenly, a flock of birds appeared from them and flew above our heads, from the main gate. We ducked as an instinctive reaction.

We went inside and were now in a big room with undone walls. One of them was half-broken and connected to another big verandah. Surprisingly, there was a small dome in the middle of this room. Sasha threw light on it; there was a little flag on top of it and a small statue of Hanuman ji inside it.

"Holy cow, what is Hanuman ji doing here?" Unnati gained courage as she broke our line and moved ahead to bow in front of the idol with folded hands. She started reciting the *Hanuman Chalisa* and gestured to us to join her.

Within the next few seconds, we were down on our knees, beside her, and joined the chorus. Though I am a non-believer, it didn't take me long to convert.

When we got up, we felt a little braver. Sasha said, "I... I think it is good we came... here... there is no... bhoot-voot or paranormal activity here."

"Yeah!" Unnati and I said, in unison.

"Let's go out now. There is nothing here," Unnati said.

"If there is nothing here, we have no reason to be scared. Let's sit and have some more drinks here!" Sasha said. I don't know where he got that courage from. Maybe his prayers were real. Like Unnati, I decided to be quiet and follow him. We sat and he poured out more drinks. I can easily say that I had never been as tired, drunk and scared than that night. It was well past midnight and going by folklore, there'd be a princess dancing somewhere between 1:00 and 5:00 a.m. Myth had it that she waited for the Prince of Ajabgarh to beat all odds and rescue her from this trap and if he did so, this haunted place would be rid of its curse.

After a good fifteen minutes, Sasha cried, "I don't want to go out now. What's the time? It's 1:30 a.m., let's just stay for another four or five hours and go out when there is sunlight. That voice was scary!"

I stared at him in horror. "You... You mean you heard it too?" I gulped from the bottle. Neat rum tasted like cold coffee.

"Of course we all heard it, Ab. I just didn't react probably thinking that I might scare you guys as well!" he said, snatching the bottle from me.

I was dead scared. It meant that somebody had really replied to Unnati's song. We still chose to stay inside this ruined palace! I settled down at my spot again and Unnati and Sasha stood beside me. We huddled together, hoping that it will be easier to die together than be attacked separately. I continued blabbering meaninglessly to them, to lessen my own fear. The eeriness of the night continued to haunt us all. There were strange noises that just didn't seem to stop. I don't know when I dozed off.

❖

After what seemed like a few minutes, I felt a hand shaking me.

I saw light through my eyelids, and heard birds chirping. With groggy eyes, I saw a young man dressed in khaki like the guard who had escorted us the previous night. He said, "I came early, fearing for you and your friends. Chander Kaka, the night guard, called me and warned me about a group of youngsters visiting the fort late at night. I am so glad that you all are okay. But there must be another friend of yours, right? You were three, right?"

We got up and saw Sasha lying in another corner of the room, as he needed more space to sleep on the floor! We thanked the guard many times, for getting there early. We then recounted our experiences to him.

Saying goodbye, we hurriedly went to our car outside. It was strangely dark brown, with dust all over it instead of its original white. We thanked him one final time before getting into the car, when he asked, "What was the sound you said you heard, Abhay?"

"Some female voice that said, 'You haven't even seen me yet!'" I said, adding that my friend had also heard it.

Sasha was confused. "But I was only referring to those sounds of the animals," he said.

The security guard came closer to me and said, "You are the Prince of Ajabgarh that our princess has been waiting for more than five hundred years now! Because you...you heard her!" he said and turned around to pick his stick and walk back inside the fort.

Sasha whispered to me, "I don't know about you, but he certainly is!" I blankly reversed my car and we drove off in the other direction.

A letter from Nani

Bhangarh to Alwar should have been the obvious choice, but intimidated by last night and the fact that I had caught up with a few hours of sleep, I decided to drive on NH-11 instead and stop at Jaipur directly.

"Yesterday was easily the longest day of my life, and the worst too!" said Unnati sitting next to me, recounting the tragic start at Amritsar and ending with the nerve-wracking chills at Bhangarh. To be honest, I had better sleep the previous night, as opposed to her. I said, "Listen, Unnati. The day is behind us now. Let's focus on the rest of our journey."

"You know, I was thinking this morning, is it worth risking our lives for an adventure? What is the point of all this? We are so close to Delhi! Let's call it quits."

"We can't do that!"

She became silent. I continued, "We have barely made it to six places so far. We have not even covered North India yet! This journey is about covering the entire country. I am not going to cut it short because we had one bad day."

"What difference would it make?" she asked, checking herself in the small mirror in the sun shade.

This time, Sasha said, "It is the only thing I am really setting out to achieve. It's all that I have to complete in my life, Unnati.

I have to live it. It is my ultimate dream, it is my mission now to finish it, more than just about leisure or fun."

She rested her head back and smirked again. "You guys are too much. If it's not for fun, then do you think Record Books will felicitate us? Or you think this handycam-shot movie will make us famous?"

"Some things in life are not just about achievements. I have been a quitter all my life – be it in sports, studies or career choices. This trip is the only thing I feel ignited about, thanks to Abhay. Please don't let it slip away. More than the others pulling me down, I will not get confidence to do something ever again if I don't finish it."

His passionate speech silenced her. Unnati blew him a flying kiss in approval. I decided to change the topic.

"Really? No one heard her? Am I the only one who did? The real Prince of Ajabgarh?" I asked.

"Yeah! Go back and rescue her! Okay, guys, at least promise me that for the rest of this trip, I get to decide what risks we can take. I will decide where we stop, and the activities that we get to do. In short, I am the captain of this ship from now on!" She sounded serious. We nodded.

"And Ab, this was our fifth destination by the way, not sixth. Corbett, Haridwar, Ladakh, Amritsar and Bhangarh!" she added.

"What? Fish! I forgot that we didn't go to Rishikesh! Damn! The pictures we took were with sign 6!" I said.

That was when we realized our folly. Due to our nervousness that late night, we had taken pictures with Sign 6 when we had entered the fort. Moreover, we had not made much of a recording inside the fort, including this morning, for an important element of my script.

"No way are we going back to that bhootiya-mahal! Either live with it, or we will just fake it in another palace at Jaipur! And yes, in the daytime only!" Unnati, the self-proclaimed skipper announced.

Her decision was wise. I kept driving till we reached Jaipur and crashed at an average hotel in the pink city's old bazaar. After the previous day's antics, it was important for us to go easy and rest our hearts.

Our stay in Jaipur over the next few days was extremely comforting. The city had a lot to offer in terms of food, something that we had not truly experienced thus far. We also had a glimpse of the unparalleled cultural heritage that Jaipur has preserved over the course of its long history. Grand palaces, markets with wares sold at very cheap prices, turban-wearing men pulling their camels and colorfully dressed women selling little hand-made stuff by the side of nearly every road – the sights and sounds of Jaipur were soothing and gave us a 'back-to-life' kind of feeling.

That night, we splurged on a meal at Suvarna Mahal – a property belonging to the Taj Group of Hotels. It was one of the finest and grandest dining experiences one could ever get. In a big dining hall with large chandeliers and even larger crockery, it felt royal, to be able to tuck into super-spicy Indian food. Turban-clad stewards served food at their gracious best. We felt like colonial visitors at a king's palace!

At two thousand rupees per head, it was expensive. But we felt so much better after the meal. Sasha was right. Food really can trigger true delight in a person.

The next day, we visited Chokhi Dhani, a famous ethnic village created on the outskirts of the city. It was more of a mela, and a better one than the Kumbh Mela, in the sense that it had activities that one could participate in. I felt better, and saw my friends enjoying themselves too. Performers and acrobats at Chokhi Dhani were finally getting the better of us as we got soaked in their makeshift entertainment den. Unnati got her fate read by a local fortuneteller when my phone rang.

"Hello," I said loudly, so that the person on the other end could hear me. It was noisy. There was no response, so I spoke up a few times. I heard the sound of breathing, and then silence, again. "Who is it, please?" I asked, worried.

I didn't expect a call from anyone. My friends had often received calls from their homes while on the trip, but they were the ones who had left a family behind for this madness, not me. Mine had deserted me long ago. Finally, the voice said after eternity, "Hello Abhay! It is me."

I recognized her immediately. "Mom! Is it really you?" I was shocked. She hadn't tried calling me for over a year now.

"Yeah. I just... I was missing you, son. I thought I would call you. How are you? Where are you these days?" she asked.

"Why? Don't you have your new husband that you have time to miss me?"

"Having a man for the second time in my life doesn't mean that I will forget my only son. Ever. Will you please let it go now?" She said, but she was not loud. She didn't even sound like she was breaking down.

"I have accepted it and moved on, too. I am very happy. Thank you for asking. So what if you left me alone in a muddle? I have my friends and have made a life out of it and it's blossoming!" I taunted and sounded almost self-defiant. Clearly, I could never let it go.

She was calm. "It's good to hear that. Beta, I was wondering if we could meet sometime. I also have some of your Nani's possessions to share with you. I know you won't come home. But can I come to yours? Tomorrow?"

"I am travelling currently. I won't be back for another two months at least. I will meet Nani and collect it from her. Thanks for offering. Listen, I am in a hurry now, bye!" I hung up before she could respond.

I stared blankly at Sasha and Unnati, who sat with the cheesy palmist. My phone beeped, signaling that an SMS had arrived. It was from her.

Abhay I kno u will nt 4gv me so easly bt it dsnt mean I will stp trying. bcz our rltnshp is frm ur brth nd wil last til my death n u cnt chng tht. bt ys whn I die, u wil miss me bt I hpe u dnt regret nt tlkng ur heart out 2 me thn, jst as I m doin nw 4 my own mom. ys, Nani is no more btwn us. she died few nites bck peacfully in her sleep. as mch as I miss her nw, I miss u evn mre. she hs sm of ur chldhood pics and a few othr thngs wrappd in a box jst 4 u whch she wishd no1 bt u to opn. pls give ur whereabouts so I cn atlst courier ths parcl 2 u. wish 4 her in ur prayers & 4gv me my son – luv mummy.

My eyes moistened when I read the message. I wasn't particularly close to my maternal grandmother, but it doesn't mean that I didn't run around her house as a child or didn't break her window-panes playing cricket. I remembered her poha particularly; it was a dish she religiously fed me every time we visited. I quickly ran to Sasha and pulled him to a corner.

"Bhai, what's the address of our hotel in Jaisalmer?" We were to leave for Jaisalmer the next day.

"What? Why do you ask? What happened?"

"I will tell you the whole story later. Tell me the address."

"I don't know. Umm, well we stay in a tent there, Ab. Remember, you said it'd be more fun to stay in the desert amidst sand dunes and camel dung?" he mocked me. I remembered that conversation. To receive Nani's parcel, I had to stretch it out further there.

I went to my car to check the itinerary. My confused friend followed me and kept asking what had happened. I grabbed our diary from the dashboard. After Jaisalmer, we were to head to Mount Abu. We had chosen to stay at an unconventional location to enjoy a bicycle excursion. Following that was Udaipur where our booking was not confirmed due to the peak season. That was then followed by a trip along Western India, to the Rann of Kutch, the Ellora Caves and a bunch of other tourist locations where we had decided to plan our stay impromptu.

"Who the fuck made this itinerary? Why didn't we book proper hotels?" I barked at him.

"You!" he replied coolly and then added, "You said we are explorers and not uncles-with-babies who look for planned holidays.

I told him about Nani. Normally, I don't have to give him much of a back story – that was the best part of our friendship. He always knew what I wanted in situations like these.

After some thought, he said, "We should be in Goa after about eight or ten days from now. Though our resort is booked there, I have a friend in North Goa who can receive this parcel for us."

"Great, matter solved! Call him and ask for his address then. And listen, take this parcel too, it needs to be couriered to Mumbai." I gave him a parcel of my own.

I then texted my mother saying,

sorry abt Nani. may her soul rest in peace. I m going to miss her too. here is d adrs – F/41, K-block, Mahim Apartments, Anjuna Beach, Goa.

I chose not to comment on our equation or her missing me. She immediately replied saying,

my son is chilling in Goa! Wow! hv fun. hv a gud life!

I put my phone inside and went back to Chokhi Dhani with Sasha to feast on their unlimited buffet.

Our drive through Rajasthan the next morning wasn't particularly pleasant. We started early in order to beat the heat. But by 8:30 a.m., the sun's sharp rays began beating down on us through the Little Beast's windows. It'd have been fair to rename 'the beast' as a cat or donkey, because by now, it was terribly over-driven and under-cared for. Therefore, its air-conditioner also was not at its best anymore. Or maybe, it was the typical Rajasthan heat that had tamed it. After breakfast at a highway joint, Sasha announced that he was going to lie down in the backseat till we reached Phalodi, a small satellite town where we intended to stop for a late lunch break on our way to Jaisalmer. It meant that I had to drive all by myself, as we didn't trust Unnati's driving.

"Listen Ab, I know you love your car too much. But believe me, you can try me. I have a proper license. Worst-case scenario, it'd get a few scratches! Besides, you will be sitting next to me!" she told me after a while.

I became shaky at the thought. "You know, every truck driver in India has a license too."

"How mean!"

"Listen, I know you can drive well. I am just giving you more time to relax, to soak in the lovely weather outside, you know, take pictures, chat and have fun."

She wrinkled her nose and stuck her tongue out. I settled back in the driver's seat. She looked cute whenever she did that.

"Chit-chat with whom? This sleepy giant!" she pointed, as Sasha was snoring loudly now, literally.

"I am not bad company."

"The last time I got to talk to you, it didn't work well. I told you to confide in a woman, that is – in me, whenever you have to pour your heart out, remember? We are better listeners and I am the queen when it comes to that. But you didn't take it, I guess." She made a face again.

"What makes you say that?"

"Yesterday at dinner. I saw that you were upset about something. Sasha was whispering to you continuously. It means he knew what your problem was about, but I didn't."

Shit! This girl was observant! And perceptive too. Maybe she was right. She may have made a better listener.

"Well," I said, "It was nothing much. Actually, my grandma passed away. I was upset because of that."

"What?" she roared.

"Yeah. But hey, it's not like she died yesterday. She probably died a few days ago. I am not even sure when it was. My mother told me last evening, so..." I tried to sound casual.

"What is wrong with you, Abhay? How can you take it so lightly? You should have been back to Delhi already to console your mother! I know that you don't get along with her, but hey, this is not the time to pick bones. Go stand by her, for her sake, and show her that you care!"

"See? This is why I don't tell you stuff. Why do you get judgmental? If she needs me now, I can't do anything about it. I have been empty without her for so many years!" I was irritated. "Anyway, my uncles and aunts are there. It's not that they even told me when it happened or called me to attend the funeral. You don't know anything about this, Unns."

"But she sounds like a nice...."

I suddenly took a sharp turn. A camel, our first sighting outside Chokhi Dhani, stood in the middle of the road. I had to apply the emergency brakes.

Unnati said, carefully changing the topic. "This is the first time that you called me Unns! Only people very close to me call me Unns."

She smiled. "I like that!" she said.

What was she trying to do? Why was she being nice to me?

The camel's owner came running and apologized. "Sorry bhaiya! This camel won't budge from his position on the road. If you honk or do anything, he may become aggressive."

"So what do we do?"

"Can you leave your car here for sometime? Please do not move. My stupid camel will go to the field by himself, shortly. Till then, you can come down to our hut there and enjoy a glass of buttermilk each!" he pointed at a hut, outside which many camels sat or grazed.

I looked at Unnati who didn't seem to mind. She got off immediately after wrapping her scarf around her head. We decided not to wake Sasha up, and left the air conditioning on. We sat on a small bench and were handed huge glasses of buttermilk. Unnati got up and starting clicking selfies, posing beside a rather bored-looking camel resting near the bench. The way she pouted to click the perfect picture, even that poor animal lit up and seemed interested.

"Abhay, come and take a picture na? I can't get a good one on my own."

I got up and pulled out my camera. "Unnati, come on! Give me some dialogues, too. Let me capture this."

"Like this?" she asked, pointing at her denim shorts and a plain yellow T-shirt.

"Yeah! You look good, Unns! Just do it." For the second time in a while, I had called her that. She smiled and said something about the weather and about Rajasthan. We took a few more pictures with the camel, bringing excitement to its otherwise seemingly mundane day. A little silver ring shone brightly on one of her fingers and I couldn't help stare at her dainty hands for a minute longer. I posed in front, capturing her behind the lens. She said, "You know, you should give your friend a few tips on how to make a girl laugh!"

"Really? But I thought you fell for his sense of humor in the first place." I asked, setting my camera aside.

"Yeah. He is good at it. But making funny jokes and making your partner laugh are two different things. I think he can learn a thing or two from you."

Now, I am always game for healthy flirting. A boy and a girl are always entitled to indulge in it, even if they aren't seeing each other. It's totally healthy and is a good way to keep one interested in their vanity. "I was born with it, I can't give it away just like that!" I said.

"At least lend it. Believe me, your friend will get a lot of benefit if you lease it for a few days."

"Let me think. So technically, it is something that I will lease to him and he will benefit from. While I will get nothing. Won't it be better if I use it myself and get to keep the goodies too?" I teased her back.

I liked that she flirted with me, to be honest. She smiled as I finished my drink. Meanwhile, the man came to us with folded hands and thanked us for letting his camel cross the road peacefully. We moved back to the car. Sasha was still asleep, so we continued with our flirting game.

"Technically, if you keep making me laugh and feel good about myself, I should give you the privilege of feeling good about yourself, too. How do I do that? Let me think. What do you like the most? Umm..." she began thinking aloud. I started the engine.

"Think, think! You should know me well by now," I prodded her.

"You like to explore new places which we are already doing. What else? You like to drink and party, which we can't do now. But I promise, we will do a lot of it in Goa. Umm, you want to be with someone, I assure you that I will be the one to fix your perfect match. You won't admit it, but I know that you like to be cared for. You want somebody to preempt your feelings and do things for you before you can ask!" she said in a breath. I was astonished. She was absolutely correct in her last observation.

"You are really good at it," I told her. Pointing to the rear-view mirror, I said, "That ass is really lucky!" I wondered if she was magically binding me too, like he did to my friend. It was late afternoon when we finally reached Phalodi. However, it didn't seem worthwhile to stop there and break our momentum. It was too hot to step out. We looked at each other and, probably thinking the same thing, decided to just keep moving. It was only after an hour or so that Sasha finally woke up and demanded to know our whereabouts.

"Err actually, we left Phalodi behind!" I told him.

"What! You guys are junk. Never follow the plan. Our new captain, Ms Toothy, what happened to you, my dear? I just took a little nap and you became like him?" he sulked making a face.

"A nap? You slept for six hours straight in a moving car! What's wrong with you, fatty? I know you don't care for the plan, you just care for your food." Unnati scolded him. I looked in the rear-view with wide eyes.

Sasha didn't bother to look at me and gave it right back to her. "Never call me fat in front of any of my friends. I told you earlier also!"

"Anyway, what do I call you? A thin guy who has extra hundred kilos on him?" She was getting worked up too.

"Buzz off, bunny!" He showed his anger and just pushed his head back. From almost making love in this car in my presence a few days ago, they were now calling each other names.

There was an uncomfortable silence after that. I chose to act like I was non-existent and just kept driving.

It was well into the night when we realized that there has been nothing but the desert on both sides for over an hour or so. However, the GPS still showed that we were far from our destination. It was then that I realized that we had lost our way, though we were rightly in the extreme west of Rajasthan. I remembered my lesson from Lonely Planet. While driving through deserts, the road may seem endless. Nevertheless, the fighting love-birds refused to speak. I saw a guy walking wearing the turban typical to the region. He had a camel by his side. "How far is Jaisalmer?" He folded his hands and said, "*Khambaghani Bhaii-sa.* You are in Jaisalmer already."

"We are actually looking for Sam Sand Dunes Camp Site. It is in village Kanoi. Can you tell me the way?"

He started laughing. "Brother, this is a desert. You can gaze for kilometers ahead at a time, and will only see sand and nothing else. To reach a camp or anything in the middle of it, you have to leave the main road and take those little bylanes on either side. Look there carefully!" he pointed out to a little by-lane on the left. After guiding us the right way, he said again, "Remember the golden rule of the desert. Don't drive after dark, there is no guarantee, you may just be passing the same spot again and again and again." I thanked him and turned my car around. As for the two angry trounced warriors, they just kept staring outside from their seats.

After navigating through the desert with great difficultywhere the GPS was truly useless, it finally seemed that the campsite was very near as we heard sounds and saw flashy lights. When we reached there, I was disappointed. It was far too commercialized for my liking.

Girls go crazy over snowfall or about taking a dip in the sea. Usually, guys like to climb up the mountains or fly in the air. Of all creations of God, I have always loved the desert, the most. I have always fantasized about sitting in the desert with nothing to do, staring at the sameness of everything around. It gave me a sense of peace to see everything around me being incredibly stable. This camp offered nothing like it though.

It was around 8:00 p.m. A bunch of folk dancers welcomed us and performed a fake aarti as we stepped down from the car while a valet from the other side bent down in greeting, bowing as low as the human spine can allow. A valet! In a desert!

I knew I was at the wrong place. What worsened the experience was Unnati's curt remark as she moved ahead of us: "I don't think you care enough for what I like, Sashank. Let me know if you are still interested in being together." She moved swiftly after that, without waiting for us to catch up.

Love is a
renewable resource

If you've ever seen a hunter who worked hard on his prey, yet just as he is about to make the killing shot, the deer lifts its head and runs away behind the bushes. The hunter's mouth gapes wide in shock and despair at the same time. That's exactly how Sasha looked, sitting on his side of the bed the next morning when I woke up.

"Ab, what did she mean by 'let me know if you are interested'? Is she breaking up with me?"

"For all you know, she may be teasing you," I said, getting up and wearing my slippers. I needed to brush, but, he didn't let me go.

"Bhai, I am worried. She never talks to me like that. We have had disagreements, but not like this." He seemed to be on the verge of a minor attack.

I sat beside him on the bed, and rubbed his shoulder gently. "Shut up and get ready. Go out and behave normally with her. I am sure she'd have forgotten your fight by now. Wish her, praise her, make her a good breakfast. She should feel that you're over yesterday's argument."

We zipped our tent open and stepped out to a bright sun. Sasha had worn his favorite T-shirt that read *'Stay Calm and don't Ignore*

Me!' He looked more like a football ready to be kicked. He never understood that he was too big to be ignored. Unnati was in no mood to let go. We saw her talking to some aunties camping opposite us. I pushed Sasha to talk to her and reminded him to be casual.

"Hi Unns, good morning!"

She didn't reply.

"Hello aunty... a... aunties!" He wished them.

They smiled and waved at him. He waved at them awkwardly. They asked me to join their conversation. I walked up to them with a bored look. However, it changed as I saw a group of really hot college-going girls and a few brash guys join them. They were their sons and daughters. They were from a club, I think Lions Club Jaipur. They had come for their quarterly excursion and had brought their families along. I really needed a break from these two, having had no other company for a couple of weeks. I was a part of their group soon. I didn't mind being among so much eye candy.

The lovers, however, continued to sulk and remain aloof as we ate the hot breakfast buffet. I wondered what was with these Rajasthani folk that made them eat such spicy food, given the harsh temperatures in their state. I discovered the answer in Sakshi, easily the best looking girl in my newfound group. She brought her plate and sat beside me while eating. Her rompers were as short as that of a toddler's, and her mother was certainly cool about it because she sat at the table next to ours. Maybe she knew about the boiling hot weather. Or maybe she used to wear them herself in her twenties. Whatever. We soon formed a friendship of sorts and I was all set to try my luck.

The camp manager had organized a ride in the desert, to be made on camelback at noon. The one hour long journey promised to take us to a point in the Thar Desert where we could see camel racing events and even place bets. Of course, it was a discreet thing and arranged without much hype. Only the younger people camping there were aware of this. More than attending the races,

I was excited about the journey and planned the advances that I could make on Sakshi during this long ride. About twenty of us gathered at the spot and were ready to get on the camels.

"Two people on one!" announced the manager. Everyone quickly started looking for a camel to climb upon and a partner. I mentally hi-fived myself as Sakshi came to me, wearing yet another micro-mini dress, and asked me to join her. I was about to climb when Unnati stood next to the poor camel, "Abhay, you have to sit with me."

"What? Err Unnati, Sakshi and I are riding this one. Why don't you find another one? Where is Sasha? Please look for one for him too," I looked at her with pleading eyes.

"No way am I sitting with him! Do you want me to sit with you or not?" she asked in a no-nonsense manner.

"It's not that! But you see, Sakshi is afraid of these animals. She spent ten minutes getting acquainted with Bhola and now he likes her too. So you see, she will feel safer with him." I had no idea what I was saying.

Sakshi stared me with blank eyes. I swear I saw her face powder fall out in reaction.

"In that case, I will sit with her on this one. You go camel-hopping with your friend." Unnati said. Without waiting for my response, she asked the helper to assist her mount the camel. Sakshi had little choice and climbed after Unnati. I stood there, watching the camel get up. It was clearly his lucky day and not mine. For the next hour, I sat on whatever millimeters of space was left for me behind Sasha on another poor camel's back. I was sure that the camel was cursing us, especially when he crossed Unnati's and Sakshi's camel. This camel ride was as good as a near-death experience. We reached the spot and got off. I smiled at Sakshi, with a tired but enthusiastic smile. She didn't react, and went back to her group.

"How was it?" Unnati asked, sounding exhausted.

"Not so bad, how was yours?" I asked.

"Yeah, it was good. We had a good time. Sakshi is fun to be with, and so was the camel."

I was happy to hear that Sakshi was fun. I was about to speak, but Unnati said, "I told her that you and me, that is, Abhay and Unnati, are a couple. She congratulated me on my choice!" She smiled and walked away.

I looked at Sasha. He offered me a resigned look and said, "Bhai, she is not only mad at me, but I think at you as well."

I had nothing to say, although I had something else in my mind.

❖

By late evening, we were so exhausted with the dust of the desert that I had to rethink my love for dry sands. In the evening, we had a bonfire and gathered with the members of the other group. Some Rajasthani folk dancers started performing and began entertaining the guests.

One of the guys said aloud, "Did we come to the desert to watch this? When I went to Dubai for the desert safari, we were treated to belly dancing. This is so boring." Everyone began to laugh. The elders made faces and the younger group started getting up to take their party elsewhere. One of them asked me, "Abhay, do you and your friends want to join us?"

I looked at Sakshi. She avoided my gaze and started talking to her friend. I said, "No thanks, we are good here and will retire early. We leave for our next destination tomorrow morning."

"Good luck with your crazy journey, dude. Tell me if you ever finish it. See ya!" he said and joined the rest of them.

One of the uncles said, "Ignore him, Abhay. What you guys are doing is amazing. It reminds me of my youth. Remember, Naresh, when we were in college, one morning I woke you and Chopra, and we went to Kashmir? It was not considered safe to go there, but it was so much fun."

His friend laughed and recalled their antics. "Yeah Raman! And you called your girlfriend from an STD booth after emptying a full bottle of whisky. How can I forget that!" Everyone started laughing, and began teasing Raman Uncle. His wife pitched in too.

"Really? But you never called me, Raman? Who else were you seeing?"

Another lady joined the session and said, "Sushma! He called me, yaar. I did not give him room because I knew you liked him. Otherwise, the scene today would have been different."

There was a huge roar of laughter. Another lady said, "But these boys don't have this problem. In our times, if parents came to know that we had planned such road expeditions with our boyfriends, they'd first get us married and then pack us on a honeymoon instead!" There was another round of laughter.

I looked at Unnati. She had to pretend to be amused, though I could read that she was still mad at Sasha. He just kept silent and ate his snacks. Raman Uncle, who had started the conversation, asked her, "Unnati beta, tell us about your love story. Come on."

Everyone started prodding her.

One of the aunties snatched Sasha's plate and made him sit next to her to hear out their story. The pestering worked and Unnati finally agreed.

"Well, Sashank and I lived in the same locality some years ago. Now we've shifted, but back then, in 2002 I think, our houses were a few meters away from each other's. He comes from a large joint family, and one of his cousins who lived in the same house became my good friend. We used to hang out together after college, sometimes at his home and sometimes at mine. Through her, I met him," she said and paused.

"Okay, but how did you actually fall in love?" someone asked. I had silently set up my camera and was recording her story.

"One day, his sister came to me, crying, saying that her marriage was arranged against her wish. She wanted to become an artist and didn't want to settle down at that young age, but their family was conservative. The only person who supported her in their house was Sashank. He tried to convince everyone, but no one batted an eyelid.

"So then, seeing no other alternative, Sasha and I went to meet the groom and told him everything, hoping to have him call off the wedding. But it didn't work and instead, caused a lot of drama. In the end, since the wedding wasn't called off, Sasha helped his sister elope and arranged for resources for her to start life afresh in another city. I was impressed by his caring nature and love for his sister. After a year or so, he made her reunite with her parents and the rest of the family. Now she works with a top magazine. She fell in love and got married, this time with everyone's permission. All credit for resurrecting her life goes go Sasha. If he sees anyone in a fix, he goes out of the way to help them. This quality is very rare and I just knew I had to be with Sasha. So I asked him out myself. Really, such guys must not be missed out on!"

She put her arm around his shoulders. Everyone started clapping. I was in disbelief. I had never expected him to be this heroic. What with the extended permissions we had to take from his family for this road trip!

Raman uncle said, "Sashank, son. Don't you have anything to say?"

His eyes became moist as he said, "I love you, Unnati. Please don't be mad at me, I can't take it!" He got up and went to his tent, crying. All the uncles and aunties became conscious of the sudden change. I gave them a thumbs-up sign as gratitude.

Career blues

There were neither birds chirping nor roosters calling to wake us up at 5:30 a.m. The desert can be pretty silent and loony. It was as if we were the only souls in the middle of nowhere at that hour. Bound by our purpose, we decided to resume our journey as soon as we could. We had no reason to visit Jaisalmer and its epic forts. Our itinerary was prepared with a mission – to cover India's cultural and social diversity and we had shot enough palaces and forts of Rajputana culture in Jaipur itself. After a day-and-a-half's camping in Thar, it was time to get behind the wheels and move to our next destination, Mount Abu. It is a small hill station located on the border of Rajasthan and Gujarat. We badly needed to get respite from the Rajasthani heat. Before going to Udaipur – where we had a royal treat waiting for us – we decided to spend a couple of nights in Mount Abu. While driving, I wondered if there ever was a more incomprehensible person than Unnati. She was totally in love with Sasha, but was busy telling people she and I were together. What was her real self? Are all women such mixed bags? Or did she have something in mind?

"I didn't understand one thing, Unnati. You were mad at him, then why did you screw it up for me?" I asked, over tea.

"Huh?"

I reminded her of how she had made a joke out of a potential 'something' between Sakshi and me.

"Dude! Get a life. She was a typical city girl. Those 'I just want to increase my Facebook friends list' type and then show off her pictures to friends saying, 'He flirted with me all through the trip, jerk!', or one who'd use easy targets like you to sponsor their expensive interests."

"How do you claim to know her so well?" I wasn't entirely convinced with her explanation.

"Why, didn't I spend an hour with her on the camel? What do you think we girls talk about? Besides, I promised you that I would hook you up with someone, remember? It was my duty to examine her thoroughly."

I wasn't satisfied. But I chose to let it go. I turned to Sashank. "Why did you never tell me about your sister? It was Komal, your younger chacha's daughter, right?" I knew all his cousins since our school days. Komal was almost the same age as us, maybe a year younger, and was a creative genius. It was hard for me to imagine what she must have gone through.

"Yeah. She is my sister, dude! How can I share her past and her secrets with everyone openly?"

I smacked him lightly on his shoulder. Though I was proud of his integrity and modesty, I still teased him. "So I am 'everyone' now? Yeah, right!"

He increased the speed and said, "Shut up! You know you are my life, darling."

It was Unnati's turn to mock him. "Hey! Then who am I?"

"You are both the most valuable people in my life. Don't make me sentimental, guys. You know how reticent I can be when that happens."

"See, this is what I don't like about you. If you care for someone, you must show it. There is nothing wrong in it. If you don't show it often, the others around you may become insecure and unsure of what you really feel," she said.

"I get it guys. I know I am bad at this. I can never bring up important matters in front of anyone. I always fall into the trap of how I will be received and worry about what the other person is thinking about me. I think purists call this a persecution complex."

"Wooo! What a nice term. Where did you get that from?" I asked.

"Google."

"Had you paid as much attention at school, you'd have been a doctor or a scientist now," I teased.

"Nah, I'd still be sitting at Counter No. 3 of Harekrishna Enterprises in Chawri Bazar, Old Delhi!" he said with a tinge of pain in his voice. Unnati sensed it too and she soothed him.

"There is nothing wrong in it. The family business is flourishing under you."

"Who are you kidding, Unns? I am just a cog in the set-up. Do you know why I work there? Because I will not swindle money from accounts as it is my family business. Otherwise, I am not needed there at all. Two of my other cousins who handle counter one and two are cool with that life, but I am not. Who am I, anyway? MF Hussain who can spill color on canvas and expect people to pay millions for it?"

I couldn't resist laughing at his comparison. Sensing that he was serious from his sober tone, I stifled my laughter quickly. He continued, "This is what my father said when I told him that I didn't want to join the business. Though I didn't have clear alternates ready, I was sure that this was not what my soul wanted. That was six years ago, but nothing much has changed."

"What do you want to do?" Unnati asked.

"I know the answer to that one!" I said. "He wanted to open a halwai shop and sit there, and sell sweets, specifically serving piping hot jalebis and samosas all day. He dreams of selling combos with tea!" I said, light-heartedly.

Neither of them laughed.

Ignoring me, Unnati said, "What's wrong with that? Guys, this is what people do in the west all the time. McDonalds, Starbucks and all those places are all results of small and personalized fast-food set-ups in their times. Why, even India has its own success stories. There are people dropping out of lucrative business careers to start up innovative teashops or cafeterias. I get to meet such people all the time at the radio station."

"They are risk-takers and had definite plans. In my case, I am nobody. I don't even know what I'd have liked to do even though opening a sweet shop was something I always fancied. Leave everything aside, what will my father think of it?"

"Bhai, for once, forget about what your father will think. It is your life. You are only twenty-five. Imagine, years later, on your deathbed, when you'd be regretting not taking this chance up to do what you want. Your father will not even be around then to feel sorry for you!" I said animatedly.

"It is easy for you to say this, Ab, because you don't care for your parents. But I do," he said.

I got upset and decided to chuck the conversation and settled back into my seat.

After a minute's awkward silence, he muttered a 'sorry', looking at me in the rear-view mirror. I knew he was disappointed about his own issue, so there was no need for me to be offended.

'Maybe it is human nature to complain,' I thought.

Would life have been different if I were in Sasha's shoes? You know, go home everyday and have so many faces to look at, however grimacing they may be. A cousin's young toddler coming to the door to greet you and hug you, and a concerned mother alongwith a couple of aunties scolding you for being late and escorting you to the dinner table. At night, there would be uncles asking for the day's ledger and collecting cash to be placed in the safe. Followed by three or four people sitting around a table in the family room playing cards, or moving out with another cousin to the market to buy paan for everyone. I don't know if I would have complained too much about sitting at Counter No. 3 all day for that life. Sure, I have been a rebel all throughout, but maybe I became one because of my folks. Had they lived together,

I'd have been a conformist myself, like him. Would I have been happier?

❖

"Why are we doing this to ourselves? Mount Abu was supposed to be a breather!" Sasha complained. He had managed to sit on a lean mountain-bicycle and pedal for a full kilometer. We had hired bikes at Mount Abu after finishing our customary rituals of taking pictures, recording voice-overs and interviewing a couple of locals. For the next day, we had only one thing on our agenda: going on a bicycle trek to Guru Shikhar, the highest point of Rajasthan. It was around fifteen kilometers from Mount Abu. Usually, people trekked to this scenic viewpoint by road. We chose to be daredevils and decided to ride on bicycles. We stopped pedaling in unison.

"You said we needed to take a break every two weeks. Is this a break or a break down?" I knew why he was shouting. Cycling, for his heavy frame, was a difficult task.

"Dude, relax! Remember you were complaining in Ladakh too? You loved it later, I said.

"My ass loved it! I lost so much fluid and Unnati became unconscious. Tell him Unns!" he barked.

"Sasha, we've only barely begun cycling. Stop being a wuss and cycle fast!" she said and dashed past us. I shrugged, and then followed Unnati. We teased him to catch up. The poor soul had no choice but to cycle behind us. After a while, when we had travelled quite a distance, and Sasha was left way behind,we decided to slow down.

Sasha finally caught up with us, huffing and puffing badly.

"Guys, let's stop for a real breather. I can see a tea stall there," he said pointing at a push-cart hidden in the bushes. The man appeared to be selling tea and Maggi. We decided to stop. After cycling for a couple of hours, we finally reached our destination only to be deceived by the view. What was promised as the highest point turned out to be a small platform of concrete. It was a viewpoint of sorts with a little hidden temple. Nonetheless, the view was a feast to the eye. Sasha decided to stay longer, as he didn't have the energy to cycle back, so we sat there, watching the little rays of the sun hidden behind the mountains ahead of us. It was mesmerizing to see how it played hide-and-seek with us and personified the ups and downs of our journey. Unnati reminded us that we had barely covered a quarter of our journey and that the real adventure was still to follow.

She asked, "Hey lovie-dovie, you had promised me something special if I stayed the night with you at Bhangarh Fort, remember? Where is my prize?" He looked at me. I winked back, telling him not to reveal the surprise, yet.

He said, "You will find it in our very next destination."

The birth of
RoadTrippers

Mount Abu to Udaipur was our easiest drive. Not only was it a mere 150 kilometers long, but also because of a smooth NH-76 that connects both cities. Udaipur was to be our last destination in north India and after casually spending a relaxing day in Mount Abu, we left for the city of lakes. Every city in our trip had at least one characteristic which separated it from the thousands of others in our country. Udaipur is popularly called the 'Venice of the East' for its beautiful lakes. Rajputana Princes considered it as their leisure valley and built many famous palaces overlooking these lakes. Now, modern hotel chains have turned them into vintage resorts, minting money in the process. Despite it being an easy road, Unnati was determined not to let us relax with her questions.

"Why am I the only one not to know what's special at Udaipur? If you both know about it, it means it's a part of the trip! Why was I kept out? Sasha, your prize was supposed to be for me! Why does he know about it already? Why?"

Everytime Sasha tried to open his mouth, I overpowered him and ensured that he didn't spill the beans. Finally, we reached Udaipur. After some navigation through the city, we reached the banks of Lake Pichola. As the icon of Udaipur, Lake Pichola was witness to innumerable tourists and obscene amounts of wealth on its banks. Every posh hotel chain owned property there and one of them even had theirs right in the middle of the Lake. Unnati got off the car and removed her sunglasses as she gaped in excitement. "It is beautiful. I want to die here!" she shouted, opening her hands in jubilation. Sasha went behind and embraced her. I had to let them enjoy their moment, so I decided to delay our customary photograph. Instead, I called up our tour organizer who arrived in ten minutes with his team.

"Why are there so many people here? What's going on? Is this my surprise?" Unnati was genuinely confused as she saw a bunch of cars stop and some people getting down with strange looking stuff in their hands.

"It has just begun. Wait and watch. Actually Sasha, she loves showman tactics, why don't you blindfold her?" I told him.

"Good idea, bhai," he said and pulled out a handkerchief to do so. Unnati had no clue what was happening. Once blindfolded, she could only hear voices as we took her hand and boarded a steamboat in Lake Pichola. Once we were in the middle of the lake, we took off her blindfold.

"Nice! So you guys wanted to give me an airy ride early morning. I am impressed," she said excitedly.

"Ab, now will you please let me say it?" Sasha looked at me.

I nodded. He said, "Darling, we are going to stay at Lake Palace tonight. All free. Actually, sponsored. We have dinner with some very elite guests right in the middle of this lake."

She was shocked and her jaw dropped. "Sponsored, did you say?" she muttered.

"Yeah! Remember, we are also making a movie out of it all? I sent some raw footage of our first couple of locations to a leading production house and they seem to have agreed to produce the movie. One of their bosses has come down to meet us for dinner and has sponsored our stay. That's not all. He even invited the representatives of the India Book of Records!" I said in one breath. Her reaction showed her disbelief. She almost fainted. When she got to her senses, she hugged us tightly.

❧

I stood in the outer courtyard of the Lake Palace. Setting up my camera on the stand, the feeling had finally started sinking in – I may actually get to release this amateur movie! It could be that something I had always wanted in life. Our dinner meeting was at 8:00 p.m. There was still time, so we decided to shoot something outside. For the first time, I saw Unnati dressed in a long, pink gown. Her hairdo was similar to that of a celebrity walking the red carpet and she wore more makeup than she had used during the entire trip.

"What are you doing, Unnati?" I questioned her.

"Why? Is something wrong? Is my dress too revealing?" she asked Sasha who stood nearby.

"No. Why are you dressed like Barbie? This movie is about three carefree backpackers and adventure travellers. You are spoiling the effect here. Sasha, explain it to her."

"You don't know these things, Ab. I work in the media and I know what these producers are looking for."

"Media? You work as an Assistant RJ, for god's sake! We never get to see what you are wearing anyway," Sasha corrected her.

"Be quiet! You don't know anything," she hushed him and started talking about Udaipur. Sasha stood next to me.

I whispered to him, "She probably doesn't know who the cameraman and editor is!" We giggled.

"You must be Abhay, hi!" A husky female voice announced from behind. I turned around to see an even more decked-up girl who introduced herself as Tanya from Bingo Productions. She was one of the 'right hands' of the main boss, or so she said on the phone.

"Well, I didn't send my pictures. You are very insightful," I told her.

"Yeah, but you said you were the one who shot this, right? Or do you just hold the camera while he calls the shots?" she asked, pointing at Sasha.

"No, it's me. Hi!" I offered my hand uneasily.

"Media, darling. We have to be on top of our game all the time. Let's go inside and grab a table!" I cursed the creator of the word media and how loosely everyone interprets it, enough to associate themselves with it.

"So Abhay, Sashank and Unnati. You have no idea of what your life can become. You may have only imagined what celebrities must be like. You are actually getting to meet one yourselves!" she said, as we settled down at a table.

"Who is the celeb we get to meet?" Sasha asked lazily and looked for someone to take his order.

She raised an eyebrow. "Well, never mind. I guess you have to work a little harder than these two. Anyway, so our boss, Suraj, will be here soon. He seldom meets newcomers himself, so be very selective and precise in what you say. Do not ask for any funding at this stage. Tell him the vibe of your movie and talk about your target audience. And yes, please tell him that you'd prefer to work with Tanya if your project is taken under his wings."

It was now becoming clearer. Was she the boss' right hand or a nail of his right hand's finger! I was losing interest. But I looked up when she said, "Here he is!"

Suraj was a young chap, probably in his late thirties. He had a certain aura around him, not just because of his popular second name – he was the youngest in the line of descendents of one of the most popular clans in the movie business. He moved everywhere with a team of people. His minions moved everyone aside and made space for him to sit right across me.

"Hi, I am Suraj Ch.." he introduced himself but Sasha cut him.

"Of course we know, sir. Who doesn't!"

Suraj beamed.

Tanya said, "Sir, he is Sashank, the food lover. She is Unnati, their voice-over model. This is Abhay, their director and the one who conceived this idea."

Suraj turned to Unnati and complimented her. "You have a very sweet voice, Unnati. You sound like a top Bollywood heroine, don't ask who."

She thanked him nervously.

"And you, Abhay. Very, very brilliant. It is only rarely in many years, if not decades, that we come across such ideas. A reality travel show is very innovative indeed! I want to know if there is more meat to it, or if it is just a concept." I became anxious. He knew how to make his meetings uncomfortable right from the word go.

"So, Abhay? Or wait, Ab?" he asked me.

"Yeah, my friends call me Ab. Sir, honestly, I am a little nervous. I don't know how to explain or where to start."

He smiled and asked a waiter to bring us some drinks. Once the drinks arrived, he got it started.

"Do you know why people watch movies, Ab?"

"For entertainment," I offered feebly.

"Yes. But entertainment is everywhere: going on a long drive or for a meal, travelling, gossiping with your friends or having sex. There are so many other nobler forms of entertainment. Why watch or make movies?"

We had no answer.

He continued, "Sitting continuously and staring at a screen for two hours and doing nothing else, but just focusing on a story. Getting drowned in it, forgetting your worries, your stress for those two hours! That's the power of movies."

We smiled in agreement.

"If your hour-and-a-half long reel is as gripping as the ten-minute footage, I assure you that we will release it. But remember what I said. The viewer must not have the urge to do anything else. It should be that captivating. I like the concept and that's why we are here," he said. I didn't know what to say. So he said, "I can sponsor the rest of your trip and make a couple of my production guys tag along."

That's when I interrupted him. "Err actually, sir. I was thinking of not using the privileges you mentioned. The nucleus of this shoot is that it is by amateur young adults on a shoestring budget. It will be lost if it becomes too grand at this stage."

"Hmm. Interesting. I agree. Tell you what, I like you man! I think we will surely release it. I will ask my team to sign up the formal contracts later today. I like things to be well documented."

We beamed in excitement and congratulated each other with our eyes. "But, you can do with some research. I will ask Tanya to be in touch with you throughout your trip and to give you inputs, etc."

My friends' smiles shortened as they heard her name. I was okay with it. I'd be okay with ten show offs like her if they released the film.

"And remember, another central part of your film is that there are three friends – two guys and one girl on this incredible journey. Neither of you must pull out at any stage or else its unconventionality is lost. Remember, if you really want your film to attract a wider audience, then commercialize it a little bit more. Tanya can give you inputs on this once the paperwork is completed. We are done!" He shook our hands as we got up. We watched him walk to the banks where he had to get into his boat.

The dream continued as the team from India Book of Records joined us next. They kept asking us the details of our preparation, our journey so far and how we intended to tide through the remaining portion as we were already half-dead and an exorbitant part of travel was virtually staring at us. The evening had pumped us with a lot of motivation. We tucked into dinner and drinks. Someone popped open a bottle of champagne and celebrated that we had already made a record of sorts by covering northern and western India in a small car. Not that they could officially record it, because it didn't fit their parameters. But they were pretty hopeful that we could finish our entire run and then establish an unassailable record. We just couldn't control our excitement. Once their team left, we partied like idiots.

After having sampled alcohol of all shapes and sizes available at their bar, I realized that I had never been more satisfied in my life.

No pat-on-the-back from my bosses or my clients in my advertising job could ever match the appreciation and encouragement I received that evening. Unnati was dancing continuously and why shouldn't she!

Sasha, poor ol' Sasha, who never in his life got a grade 'A' to boast of in front of his family, now had so much to show.

As a parting word before we retired to our rooms, Unnati reminded us, "Guys, all said and done, this is not what we came on this trip for. Remember that when we resume our journey tomorrow."

"Come here Unnati! Give me a hug and stop being a lecturer all the time," Sasha said and fell into her arms like a madman. I laughed at their awkward hug. It was like a petite toddler hugging her teddy bear. They started kissing passionately and aggressively soon. Even after what seemed like an hour, their mouths couldn't be separated from each other's. I decided that I had seen more than I should have, so quietly walked away, assuming that their party was now their own.

❖

My mouth felt dry. Despite being super tired, I just couldn't sleep. Alcohol was dancing inside my veins and I had to sit or lie down. Otherwise, I was likely to fall down. I had never felt so sloshed before, but the events deserved so.

However, my mind was elsewhere.

To be honest, it was stuck on their kiss.

The way they grabbed at each other and expressed their passion – it sure had been a sight. I had seen them get a little intimate earlier as well, so it was nothing new, but blame it on their fervor or my drunken state. I felt strange sensations just thinking about them. Here was a guy, evidently overweight, and little balding, who liked to binge and do nothing else in his life. Sure he was my best friend, but he was clearly a bit of a loser as well. And then this girl, pretty in her own way, and with a voice sweeter than the cuckoo. If she'd go purely on her looks, she can easily pick on the best guy in a crowd of a hundred.

Why was I thinking of all this? What was wrong if my best friend was kissing his girlfriend? I scolded myself as I tossed in bed. Then, the sound of Unnati's infectious laughter sounded in my ears. It was the most uninhibited way in which a person could laugh and I loved that about her. I remembered the day when Sasha had introduced her to me some years ago at his house party. It was one of his cousin's mehendi functions, and Unnati was dressed in an orange-pink lehenga, looking beautiful. For a second, I was happy for Sasha. But when she laughed at a stupid joke, I was blown away. I knew that I had to get friendly with her. When I had planned this trip, my soft suggestions to Sasha made him ask Unnati to come along. At that point, I rationalized to him and to myself that we needed her voice for the movie, and that it was good to have three people so that two of us wouldn't bore each other to death. Sasha could also stay with his girl for a long time, uninterrupted.

Back then, I didn't realize that I was saying all this for my sake. I wanted us to become good friends so that I could spend more time around her. I know why I did that. I was secretly in love with her! Now her little flirting or my reaction to them throughout the trip started making sense to me, ironically, in my drunk and senseless state. With my best friend's girl! Shit, this isn't happening.

"No. No. No. Noo. No!" I shouted aloud, getting up on my feet and walking inside my room like I was crazy. My luxurious surroundings weren't a consolation. It was hard to face my desires. But I also realized that she must be now lying under another man, making love to him, kissing him and gently falling asleep in his arms. And I was here alone in this room, sulking, insanely jealous and incomplete. I sat on the floor, rubbed my eyes and ruffled my hair. I had to get this out of my system. I held my head and stared at the floor. I didn't realize when I drifted off to sleep.

Kutch *nahi dekha,*
toh kuchh nahi dekha

"**W**hy the hell did you not park your car properly? I can see that it's a bad omen!" Unnati shouted at me the next morning as we returned to the banks of Lake Pichola. The Little Beast, my car, had two flat tyres staring at us. They looked so bad that it was obvious someone had deliberately deflated them.

"*Bhaisaa*, you shouldn't have parked your car here in the open. These hotel workers are scoundrels!" The good boatman told me politely. It was odd to hear the words 'brother' and 'scoundrel' in the same sentence and that too in a friendly city like Udaipur. I guess the Maharaja-like hospitality we received the previous day had ended, and perhaps the hotel staff had punctured our car tyres. Unnati didn't think they did wrong. The car was parked right next to a 'No Parking' sign.

And so after an excruciating wait for another couple of hours, we finally shifted our butts out of, possibly, the most important city in our itinerary. We even skipped our rest day planned there to quickly unravel the exciting challenges that had now unfolded for us.

It wasn't entirely pleasant, though, as memories of the previous night's kiss between them kept recurring. I found myself staring at her from the corner of my eye when the mechanic worked on the deflated tyres. When Sasha smiled at her sloppily, I noticed. He posed for a picture that she took on her phone. I noticed that too. When she teasingly mock pushed him into the lake, I wished that she had pushed him for real. When they asked me to join in a group selfie, I deliberately stood in the middle and looked sulky. We had barely moved a few miles out of Udaipur when Sasha demanded a tea break. Unnati asked, "Why do you need so much of it?"

"Somebody really drained my energy levels yesterday. I need to refuel!" he replied. She smiled. I didn't want to participate in the lame conversation and so silently parked the car. I went next to Unnati as Sasha went to place his order,

"Last evening after Suraj left, Tanya was talking about you," I said.

She became excited again. "Really? What did she say?"

"Well, from the rushes I sent, she felt that you stood out with your voice and personality. She sensed that you have an amazing screen presence and maybe a career in showbiz ahead of you. She added that you have to be a little more serious in your approach. After all, it will be a Bingo Productions Movie later." I tried to sound as casual as I could, lying through my teeth all this while. Tanya was too self-courteous to say anything about anyone else. Unnati was delighted and promised that she would give her best. She forced me to do a shoot right there and not care about the tea that Sasha had to drink all alone. We quickly set up the equipment and I captured some shots.

From the one-inch viewfinder of my camera, she looked beautiful. Her charm bowled me over again. I came up with a devious plan – I had to induce my best friend's break-up with this girl, by hook or by crook.

'But he is your best buddy!'

'But she is the love of my life too.'

'Come on, till yesterday you didn't even know that you love her. Now you are so sure that she is the one, for life. How convenient!'

'Love. You can tell. Sometimes you can fall in love at first sight, sometimes it can take ages to realize it, but it always happens in an instance.'

'Forget about it. Anyway, what about your friend?'

'My friend just treats her like a girlfriend, like an affair. He isn't serious about her. He will understand it. Besides, they are not good for each other in the long run. Remember, she was flirting with me on the way to Jaisalmer when he was dozing off. She even ensured I didn't hook up with Sakshi, because at some level, she too likes me, but hasn't realized it yet. Besides, they both take it as a casual thing at best.'

There were those devil-and-angel miniatures dancing in front of me and having this debate. As it usually happens whenever anyone faces such a dilemma, the devil won.

We reached Bhuj after an exhausting day-long drive on our country's pencil-thin roads called national highways; but not without our shares of troubles. Maybe Unnati was right. It was a bad omen to start the day with punctured tyres. First, we missed the cut near Radhanpur. That cut was supposed to merge and change from NH-14 to NH-15. It took us a while to figure out the correct way after that and stressed us out a lot. After asking a lot of passers-by, a truck driver showed us the correct route – but not before we agreed to sponsor his lunch at a dhaba on the way!

Our plan also turned out to be a little weak as we were told in Bhuj that evening that it takes a special permit from Bhirandiyara village to enter the Rann of Kutch, which could only be taken during daytime. Though we intended to have a breather at Bhuj and then drive straight to the Rann, Plan B had to be put into motion. We decided to spend a night in the epicenter of the 2001 Gujarat earthquake. The next morning, we headed to Bhuj.

'Kutch *nahi gaya to kuchh nahi kiya!*' (If you didn't go to Kutch, you didn't do anything in your life) read a little board hanging outside the check-post where we had to get permission from.

"Bhaaisa, it is very hot now. Why don't you people come in the evening and catch the sunset instead?" suggested the policeman heading the checkpoint.

"Sir, we are travellers and not tourists. We have a long journey ahead after Kutch!" I explained our itinerary and proudly showed off our collaboration with Bingo Productions for this project. After that, he didn't even ask for our original IDs and even gave us ideas for the shoot and some good reviews of the Rann of Kutch for the shoot outside his commandment. Thanking him for his support, we embarked on our journey of fifty kilometers to the white desert.

As we drove that distance, the scenes around us began changing. Unnati and Sasha rolled down their windows in excitement, though it was forty-five degrees centigrade outside. I couldn't stop them. I became witness to possibly the best submerging of a picture as rows of small brick-houses and huts suddenly disappeared, paving the way for a barren white land. The transition was so sudden. For a moment, we had to stop the car at that exact point and step down so that we could believe what we were seeing. Some guidance from a passerby finally put us onto a narrow lane and we realized that we were in the middle of the Rann of Kutch. The road beneath us began changing colors too. Suddenly, the car stopped. I put my foot on the accelerator and pushed hard, but it just didn't move. Within seconds, the engine stopped, too. Sasha opened his door to get down. He screamed loudly, "Oh no!"

He hastily got into the car. His feet were wet and dirty. "Ab, we are in middle of marshy lands, I think!"

"How can it be? It's a salty desert!" Unnati leaned in front as she checked out his legs.

I was worried. As usual it was useless to expect them to think of anything, so my first reaction was to take out my phone and Google marshy wet surfaces. Sadly, it was a border area and so there were no signals whatsoever. To help, however, a couple of people, probably from a tour-agency who spotted our car, came running and stood about twenty or thirty feet away from us. One of them shouted, "Guys, you need to get out of the car. Now!"

I opened my window and roared back, "We aren't waiting for pizza delivery either! How do we step out? It's all wet?"

They were too kind to ignore my mean joke. They quickly arranged a rope and started throwing one end to the car. After a few attempts, I caught it and one-by-one, we started moving through the gooey-sand. I was knee-feet deep in it, but didn't think too much about anything till I was standing outside. It was funny because it had appeared all-white only until till a few moments back. But underneath all that white was real black quicksand.

We were exhausted and dirty. We thanked the helpful locals. "Shit, I need to take a bath!" Unnati said.

The greater and harsher reality dawned on us when I saw the car there! It was one thing to get out of that mess, and another to get the Little Beast out. I stood with a worried expression and with a hand on my head, and looked at my friends. The guides were smarter. It must have been an everyday thing for them as one of them called a crane company on his walkie-talkie.

"Relax. Their crane shall be here in less than fifteen minutes. It is nearby, luckily. Just pay them directly and they will take your car back to Bhuj!" he said.

"Does it happen everyday?" Sasha asked, still panting from his efforts in getting out of the swamp.

The man laughed and said, "No, not often. But, since it can happen, the BSF has a crane operator stationed nearby. Most visitors to the Rann come with guides or someone experienced."

I sensed he was mocking us. We deserved it too perhaps.

"Anyway, guys, our resort is nearby. Once you fix your car and arrange for it to be taken back to the city, you can come over and take a wash." He pointed to a small building at some distance. Everywhere else, there was barren, white land.

We thanked them and waited for the crane to arrive. After a couple of hours in the afternoon heat, the car was pulled out and we managed to collect our bags from it before waving it goodbye to a mechanic's workshop in Bhuj. The bad omen that Unnati had pointed out the previous morning was finally showing its full form.

"We have seen it all, haven't we?" Sasha said slowly, with a lump in his throat, as we walked under the burning sun towards the building. He stopped and sank to the ground. Maybe he really was a loser.

Luckily for us, an open jeep with one of those tourist guides stopped next to us. He was escorting some of his guests back to the resort after an afternoon safari and signaled to us to hop on. We sat still, as though we were mannequins. After a refreshing bath and some rest in the resort, we were back to our senses and crashed to the open-air cafe to watch the sunset.

We had read and heard so much about it, and despite no Plan B in place, about our next move, there was no choice but to sit there and soak it in. I told my friends to let the camera be and decided not to record anything for the rest of our stay at the Rann of Kutch. Not that our mood guaranteed a good shoot anyway. With a chilled mocktail in hand and so many challenges ahead of us, I decided to dump my worries and just melt into the visual delight. It was still very hot, due to the high temperature and the blowing wind. But as the orange light started descending on the white cloud-like sand, the view was like something out of the olden time episodes of the *Ramayana* and *Mahabharata*.

My mind began running with thoughts. My distance from my mother was justified, but was it fair to keep away from grandma? Was it wrong to love Unnati just because she was my friend's girlfriend?

I heard them laughing behind me. I turned around. They were feeding each other French fries. Sasha's mouth was full, but he was still willing to eat more. She dipped a bunch into ketchup and stuffed them in his mouth aggressively. His eyes almost popped out and that made her laugh again uncontrollably.

I am going after her, I told myself.

Wrath of the devil

"**H**ello, hi! Is this Tanya? Tanya! How are you? Listen, this is Abhay..." I called her, albeit a little hesitantly. Sasha and Unnati stared at me as we stood at the small mechanic shop in Bhuj. "Yeah, the movie is shaping up well!" I said in haste, again to be stared at hard by my friends.

I then realized what I was saying. "Err... Actually no. We are in a bit of trouble. That's why I had to call you!"

I went on to explain about how my car had got stuck in the swamp and was now parked in a garage in a hot Gujarati city. I was starting to really hate their hot climate by now.

"Well, really? You can do that for us? Thanks! It will be a great help...Really?...Yeah it is white! A Ford EcoSport. Thanks so much again...Okay, I will wait for your call...Sure, please text me the name of the place and we will go and take some shots there." I hung up.

"So?" Sasha asked.

I didn't answer him. Unnati tugged at my sleeve. I smiled. "Guys, Tanya says that we are the stars of a Bingo Productions movie, after all. So what if our car broke down? They are going to arrange a white EcoSport for us in Ahmedabad!"

"What?" Unnati shouted.

"Yeah, and she is just sending me the name of an agent nearby who will arrange to drive us to Ahmedabad too. All we have to do is just make a good film."

Unnati hugged me in excitement. I couldn't forget that moment. I wish I had a way to capture memories, emotions and feelings – only to replay them and feel them all over again.

She lifted her head, still holding me tight, and said, "You are really a rockstar, Ab!"

Once my moment was over, I spoke to the garage owner and arranged for a logistics-company to deliver my Little Beast back to Delhi safely. In the meantime, Sasha got a taxi. "Come on gang! Let's go to get the surrogate beast!"

Our journey to Ahmedabad was, however, not an average ride. As a novel element in the movie, Tanya wanted us to make this 300 kilometer ride on the back of a truck and had arranged for one in Bhuj. Reading about a 300 kilometer odd long truck ride out of a marathon 10000 kilometer journey is one thing; experiencing it is another thing altogether! A mathematician would call it a 3% variance. But, it was a lot more than that for my city-bred buttocks. We had to ask our driver to stop after every fifteen minutes to take a break. For those seven or eight hours, I forgot about everything and had just one priority – to survive the ride. Sasha had the worst of it all, as he vomited twice and though his frame required every gram of food that it could get, he had to ditch lunch and snack-stops, lest he vomit again. Unnati was less perturbed. She kept our spirits high and offered some good visual shots for our film. She managed to make the truck ride look like an experience worth trying.

Disclaimer: Please don't try it, ever! Not on an Indian highway, at least.

❖

After spending the night in Ahmedabad, we embarked on our own to Unnati's favorite destination – the Ellora Caves. The only reason I could think of including Ellora in our itinerary was that it was roughly between Gujarat and Goa, although a small detour was required to actually reach it. Once Sasha learnt about it, he became excited and explained that it was a world heritage site. As luck had it, history-buff Unnati became a part of our plan, making our detour to Ellora mandatory.

"What are the Ellora Caves all about?" I asked Unnati, as Sasha drove.

She adjusted her hair for the camera. She looked into the lens and spoke, "The Ellora Caves were built around 1600 years ago. It is a formation of Hindu, Jain and Buddhist temples, showing how these cultures and religions existed in harmony. But more significant is the fact that these caves were hewn out of huge stones of the Sahyadri mountain range. It is among the largest rock-hewn complexes in the world! Imagine the kind of artistry and craftsmanship that prevailed – with mechanisms to create such monolithic structures out of rocks."

Sasha yawned loudly. History doesn't have an appeal for most men. She tapped her head lightly.

"See that's why I tell you to not shoot when he is around! He is not interested in recording any information about any of the places we visit. He just wants to know how much potato went into making a samosa!" she complained.

I butted in. "I know! That's why he wanted to become a halwai. Anyway, you go on!" Unnati was happy and gave me more information. I tuned out, because I couldn't bear that much history either – but I recorded it all. Once she was done, she pulled Sasha's cheek and said, "Poochie. You really wanted to become a halwai? My laddoo making a laddoo!" She started teasing him.

I sensed an opportunity, so I joined in. "Yeah! I remember once in college, he made something with bread and stuffed it in a large tiffin box. Then, he put it on a table in the canteen and offered it to everyone. Later on, he revealed that he had made those bread pakodas himself!"

"Then what happened?" she asked.

"Nothing! One guy said, 'Oh! I thought we were eating some continental dish!' The entire canteen burst out laughing. I still can't forget that incident."

Sasha was visibly embarrassed at the mention of that episode. I loved it.

Unnati kept pulling his leg. And I too chipped in from time to time, also adding how he was lucky enough that at least they had a settled business where he could be of use, etc. Otherwise, given his atrocious dream-job, he was bound to be a failure. Till some days back, we used to discuss alternate career options for him. It is strange how your best friend becomes a target just like that.

We reached Ellora late at night. It was a minor setback in the sense that we had no bookings. The little fiasco at Kutch meant that we were a day behind our schedule. Instead of driving to Aurangabad and returning the next day, we decided to check in at a small motel (calling it hotel will be too generous) right near the caves.

"You will be staying at roadside lodges with noises of trucks all night!" I remembered Sasha's uncle's words of wisdom when I first went to see him as I tossed around in bed. It wasn't exactly the sound of trucks, but all sorts of strange noises, and it became impossible to sleep after a while. I kicked the snoring Sasha on his back and woke him up.

"Dog! What do you want?" he barked at me.

'Your girl friend' I wanted to say but settled for, "Bhai, I was thinking about you and Unnati…"

He turned around and opened his eyes, "What about us?"

"Don't get me wrong. But I was thinking that she has completely changed you. I remember you used to drink like a fish when we had night outs back at home. And now, we've barely drowned beer twice or thrice throughout this trip. I bet after marriage, she will turn you into an uncle!" I said.

"No man. It's not about her, Mr Producer. You keep telling her to take this movie and this shoot seriously. Of late, the two of you have become so serious about this whole thing that you've forgotten that it was a fun trip to begin with. That's why I had to mellow down!" He got up.

I prodded. "Agreed, but I still see a sense of obligation to ask her. You seek her permission with your eyes and with your mannerisms before doing anything. Maybe I am reading too much into it, but I want you to remember that you shouldn't lose yourself!"

"First you suggested to her that she should dominate me. Now you say that she dominates a lot!" he asked back.

"That advice was for a girlfriend who genuinely missed her man's attention. This observation is to a brother, my best friend!" I said in a sappy way.

He became emotional, got up and hugged me. In other words, crushed me under his weight.

"Bhai, we will make up for it in Goa. We are going to burn it down, there will be beer overflowing on the streets. I love you man!" He kept hugging me. Thankfully, he let go after a few minutes and went back to sleep.

"Sasha," I said again as I lay down on my side of the bed. "Let's go to a rave party in Goa!"

He showed a thumbs-up from the other side.

❖

The visit to the Ellora Caves can be described as beautiful and mesmerizing, and a tribute to the workmen who created it over the years manually through hard work and without any modern tools. For someone like Unnati, it could also be described as a life-numbing experience as she ran through some of those temples. Even the destroyed sections left an indelible impression on her. To top it all, it looked all the more elegant through the camera.

As beautiful as the caves were, on a personal level, it was nothing but a walk through the scorching heat. The heat of

Rajasthan and Gujarat had taken its toll on us. Staring at one sculpture after another under that blazing sun was too much after an hour or so. After a while, they started looking the same. Given Unnati's enthusiasm and the need for a worthy shoot, we kept going through the motions for a good three hours!

It finally took a mild sunstroke on Sasha's part for her to call it quits. He had lost a lot of fluid and lay down on the steps of a temple due to it. The visitors around us thought he had overeaten and fallen half-dead or something. I made him drink a few bottles of Pepsi to help him regain his senses. He shouted at Unnati when he was revived. "Enough, Unnati! I am not staring at these rocks anymore. We need to go back right now." It seemed that my previous night's provocation had worked. She was taken aback, but decided not to challenge him. We took our selfie with Number 11 outside one of the temples. Besides the background, our expressions made it the most memorable photograph of all. Sasha wore an angry look. Unnati looked like a wounded tigress. I chose to go sober and wound up looking confused. Anyone staring at us taking that picture would have probably paid us a million dollars to get a copy.

We embarked on another ride to India's number one destination for chilling out, holidays and weekend breaks. Casinos, beaches, tall Russian women smoking marijuana and trolling about: Goa was the destination to be! It was my fifth visit, although this time, I had a new friend tagging along – the devil! Of late, he had become my best buddy and despite a warning the other day, he played my thoughts continuously. I had decided to cause a stir in Sasha and Unnati's relationship in Goa. This devious plan had occupied my mind throughout this drive. I paid no attention to shooting. It had become a ritual by now to stop three or four times between cities and take random shots of small towns or local shops like a barber's salon or a hawker selling clothes on the roadside. There were no stops on this stretch. We took breaks, but they were only to dine and pee. Another reason that made it awkward was the little fight our couple had in Ellora. They chose to sit silently and wear grumpy expressions most of the time. It was familiar, but this time, I let them be. It helped me relax and warm up to a bigger blow. After numerous debates between the devil and me, it was clear that Unnati had to get Sasha out of her system first before she could start considering me. I had to first cause that stir and Goa gave me the opportunity.

"Look guys, I know you are not talking to each other. It happens in a long journey and in every relationship. But for the sake of our movie, can you please play along? I know you will anyway make up in a day or two." I lectured.

"It isn't happening so soon this time, till he learns to respect me. Anyway, you are right, we need to be more professional," said Unnati.

"Exactly!"

"Abhay, I will Google some of the stuff once we are in Goa and have better connectivity. We can have some more footage of the unexplored territories besides Calangute Beach, Baga Beach, Aguada Fort, Dolphin tour, Colva Beach and Fisherman's Cove restaurant."

"I have heard that there is a nude beach in Goa where foreigners walk topless. Maybe you can shoot them too, minus the view of course," she said from behind.

Sasha's eyes went wide as he heard the word topless.

We reached Goa by late afternoon and drove to Sasha's friend first, to meet him and collect my parcel. Unfortunately, he had to go to Pune for some urgent work, but my parcel was intact with his wife.

It felt strange as I picked it, as if I was holding my Nani's hand. I decided to open it in private when Sasha and Unnati wouldn't be around. I kept it safely in the dashboard and headed straight to our resort. It was fun, as we went to Calangute Beach, straight after checking in. It was more delightful to play in the water even in the hot weather. The sight of thousands of tourists even in the peak April heat validated Goa its status as the top tourist destination of our country. After riding the water scooter, and going on the banana boat ride, followed by a round of parasailing and splashing water on each other, we were well spent. I could see that dirtying each other with sand, Sasha and Unnati were back being an inseparable couple, holding hands and teasingly hugging and pushing each other.

They let a fight die so easily! I wondered if my plan could really do them apart.

"Sasha, let's go grab a beer and some snacks buddy. I am dying of hunger." I pulled his hand and made him go with me, leaving Unnati alone on the beachside.

She got up angrily and said, "Hey what happened to you, Ab? That is usually Sasha's line!"

He laughed back and asked, "What do I order for you, baby?"

"Some seafood! Listen, you guys go ahead, I am going to change into something dry." She went while we walked to a shack.

"You two cool now? Just for the record, it was your second major fight since this trip started. Are you really sure about each other?" I asked him.

"Yeah! I had to apologize a lot. Actually, I am a fool. I was at fault. I mean, we drove down almost a thousand kilometers to those caves. And I couldn't bear walking for a few hours?" he said.

"If you are uncomfortable, then you are. You have every right to voice it out. See, you need permission to do anything. If you don't, she can easily condition you into believing that it was needed. For example..." I trailed off.

"Come on, say it!"

"Leave it, bhai. There is no use of saying anything to you. You are blindly in love, and it is okay. Just don't regret it later!" I shrugged, settling into a cane sofa at that little shack that was playing loud Bollywood music. The sun was setting, and I stared in its direction.

"Ab, just say what you were saying! You know how I always follow you." He pleaded with me, while asking a server waiter to get the seafood platter and a couple of beers at our table.

"Did you notice that you just ordered a seafood platter? For all three of us? Without asking what I wanted or what you yourself want? Without even asking for the menu? As far as I know, food is your biggest passion and yet you don't even care about what you want to have."

"It is such a petty thing. Of course, we will order more later, na?" he said casually.

I poked further, "It is not. This is exactly what I mean. It has become your second nature now. While this food order is a small thing, you are not realizing the bigger compromises you are making and will probably be making in the future."

"Tell me more," he said, sounding concerned.

"Well, the Ellora incident you just mentioned is the latest case in point. Tomorrow, I can bet on this, you will have the urge to seek her permission to go to our rave party. She will either refuse or want to join in. I totally see it coming." He looked guilty. This was my cue. "See I told you, my *chaddi-buddy!*"

"Bhai, all three of us came together on this trip. What's wrong in asking her to tag along?" he defended.

"What if she says no? Worse, what if she tells you that you can't go too because there will be drugs and there may be naked girls dancing and stuff?" I questioned him back.

He had no answers. I continued, "See, this girl can bring the nude beach in a conversation by her choice, but will not let you go to a rave party. If you don't believe me, try it out!" I pointed at Unnati. She walked up to us and settled in another chair. She had changed into a super sexy bikini and had draped a loose sarong around her body. I couldn't help checking her out. Sasha didn't care about her dress, though she tried to make him notice. Finally, she gave in and asked, "So, what have you ordered?"

Sasha tested her himself. "Chicken skewers and doner kebabs."

"But I asked you to order seafood. We are in Goa now, not Punjab. Get over chicken, foodie!" She looked for a server waiter and told him to bring her the menu. I rolled my eyes at Sasha.

"Baby?" he said.

"Yes sweetheart?" she said, busy reading the menu.

"We just got tipped about an underground party nearby. It's tonight," he whispered softly. Unnati sat up.

"What is this about?"

"There is this huge dark ground nearby. It's an abandoned area, actually. So one of the clubs is organizing a nice party. There will be laser lights, live DJs and more. It's a very discreet kind of a party," he said in a low voice. I don't know why he spoke so softly, though. Everyone is coming to Goa to visit these places, or at least hoping to know about them.

She said it loud though, "You mean a rave party?"

"Kind of..."

"Sasha, do you even know what they are about? Haven't you seen them in the movies? They will drug you there! Are you nuts? Nobody is going to visit one. Do you get it?"

A defeated Sasha lay back with a deadpan expression on his face while I remained quiet. Meanwhile, our food had arrived. Unnati got up and excused herself. She had to wash her hands (again).

When she left, I pounced on him. "See? Didn't I tell you?"

He said nothing. He kept drinking his beer while I did all the talking. "Sasha, I agree with whatever she said. Drugs are not our scene, man. But tell me, has Unnati been to any of these parties before that she'd know about it? We know that drinking is bad, so should we stop drinking? Or even going to buy liquor? Most importantly, will she decide where you can go and where you can't? Of course, we are not going to do drugs. But this girl has your pulse in her hand and knows how to tame you and make you dance to her tunes."

He finished his beer in one gulp after that and put the bottle back.

And then he told me, "Abhay! Find out about the best rave party in Goa. Only the two of us will go there."

❖

Over the next couple of days, we went to the tourist locations around. Some of the best shots were taken near Aguada Beach at the fort, which was famous for a make-believe story of two lovers dying for each other many years ago. We danced and dipped in the water at all the beaches. We drank more beer than one would in a year. We also went to a casino in a yacht and made some money. It seemed like a good omen for things to come. There were other interesting anecdotes, too. However, the final blow happened on our third and final night.

"Sashank, listen to me. I've found out about a real party, man! It is at Varca, down south, though. It starts every Friday at midnight and wraps up early on Saturday morning."

"Great!" he said. We had finished dinner and were relaxing by the hotel's poolside.

"Do we go ahead or not?"

"Of course we do."

"How?" It took a while for him to realize that it was our last night in Goa. He told me his plan. "You instruct us authoritatively that since it's our last night, let's call it early to get enough rest. Once we are off to our rooms, Unnati will probably watch TV and sleep. We will step out and return early morning tomorrow. Tomorrow morning, I will fake a headache as an excuse to start late. She will curse me for it, but I will handle her. Simple!"

It really did sound simple. After a while, I told them that we needed to start at 7:00 a.m. the next day and that everybody must pack and get ready. Unnati had no reason to suspect anything and hugged us goodnight before heading to her room. We tiptoed outside and settled into our car.

"Bhai! It's so much fun this way. I love it already," he said, excitedly, as I switched on the ignition.

"Let's make it a memorable night for brothers only. Let me grab some drinks on the way as well. It's almost one-and-a-half hours away. Wait, I will be right back!" I stepped out of the car and went inside the resort again. I went to the reception and saw a bored-looking trainee standing behind the desk. "How may I help you sir?" he asked me.

"Listen, buddy. You can help me, indeed."

"Yes sir!"

"My friends and I are staying in Rooms 201 and 202. I have to head out somewhere for something and my lady friend in 202 doesn't know about it. So if she panics and calls or comes here to enquire, please give her this address. Also, please arrange a cab for her, without even her asking for it."

"Certainly, sir. I will do that. What do I tell her, like who gave me this address?"

"You don't have to tell her anything. Just say all the young guys and girls staying in the hotel have gone to this party. And then... suggest to her that your friends must have gone to it as well," I said, as he gave me a confused look. "Listen, don't think too much about this. Here!" I handed him a piece of paper with the address written on it, along with five hundred bucks. Money can make anyone shut up. That poor chap didn't feel the need to ask me for my name anymore.

He shook hands as if he had concluded the most important deal of his life. I went back to the car with a bottle of Teacher's, and a couple of glasses. Sasha's eyes beamed as he saw the bottle in my hand. I usually don't drink whisky and he knew it well. Sasha was drinking like a fish, but I drank slowly on the pretext of driving. He shouted at the peak of his voice as he saw the venue.

"I love you, Goa! What a party man!" he kept howling as I parked the car. It was a huge area and a grand party with music blaring loud and a slew of Indians and foreigners alike. We made our way through the crowd to a dance floor and grabbed some more drinks on the way. Sasha was thumping his head now and his moves clearly indicated his drunken state. I quietly took out his mobile phone, which I had carefully picked up from the time we got off the car and gave Unnati a missed call. It was 12:30 a.m. After a minute, I gave her another missed call and then another. Suddenly, Sasha saw me fiddling with his phone.

"What bhai? You have work at this hour? Come! Let's daaance, Ab. Woooooo!" He pulled me and I put the phone into my pocket.

I now knew that damage would be done in the next few moments. I excused myself after twenty minutes from his dancing embrace for a breather. I first took out his phone. There were eight missed calls from her. I then checked mine. There were four missed calls exactly five minutes after the last one to Sasha. I played the story in my mind – *Unnati must have thought that her boyfriend wanted some romance alone and called her once Abhay had slept. However, when he didn't pick up, she became anxious and called Abhay. When both of them didn't pick up, she called our room's landline number and went there to check on us. Panicking, she went down to the reception where that guy gave her the address and arranged a taxi for her.*

Now, assuming all this had happened a few minutes ago, Unnati would be at the venue in the next hour or so! Just then, there were more missed calls from her, on both our phones. There were text messages.

I went back to Sasha who was oblivious to all this and having the time of his life, performing moves that should probably redefine the concept of dancing. I told him, "This party is so good! See! There are no drugs or people smoking either. I wish there were a few girls at least."

He raised his hand and waved at a couple of girls dancing right in frontof us. While I was away, Sasha had been fooling around and making eye contact with them occasionally. He walked up to them and introduced himself in his drunken state. The girls didn't bother; they were probably high themselves. After a while, one of them was dancing close to me and I could see that the other was totally into Sasha. Suddenly, I saw them kissing. I don't know who had initiated it, but there they were. I so wished Unnati would arrive right then!

"Hey do you wanna do it too?" the girl with me smiled as she saw me looking at them. I returned her a half-smile and just grabbed her by the waist to dance closer to her. Sasha came to me. He seemed knocked out. "Bhai, Sonali wants to show me something in a quieter space. I suggested we could go to our car. What do you say?" He was almost falling while speaking. Sonali and I had to hold him by his shoulders while walking outside. The other girl walked beside us. Sasha and she had barely settled into the back seat of the car that they started kissing again. Though these girls weren't attractive, they were certainly advanced. I had not expected her to be this desperate to kiss this potato!

Once they broke their kiss, she took out a pouch from somewhere, opened it and started inhaling from it. Without an invitation, Sasha did the same. Drugs! These girls were there to either sell them or get guys to become addicts. The girl beside me smiled continuously, expecting me to make a move. My phone vibrated again. I took it out and saw Unnati's name flashing. I stepped out of the driver's seat immediately and took the call.

"What the hell, Ab? Where have you guys been?" she shouted. I tried to calm her down, but she didn't listen. "Tell me exactly where you guys are!"

I saw a white Indigo parked ahead. Her head poked out. She stepped out angrily, but was taken aback looking at the dark girl in shiny clothes. As her eyes met mine, I just bowed down and pointed at the car. She went in and saw Sasha inhaling the drugs with a girl. Unnati's world collapsed. She sat down on the floor while I went running to help her back on her feet. Sasha saw her and his eyes popped out. He stepped out too, while the girls quickly disappeared. Unnati sat on the ground, holding her head while I splashed water on her. Sasha and I made her lie down on the back seat and were soon driving back to our resort.

Volcano in Mysore

Dear Abhay,

You are reading this letter and it means a lot to me. It also gives me satisfaction that you still care for your old granny, despite your strained relationship with your mom over the last few years. Of late, I have been keeping unwell and am mostly confined to bed. Usually, these are times when we oldies miss their relationships the most. I wish that our dear ones could be with us all the time. However, these are also times when our dear ones are busy making their lives for themselves.

It's a funny paradox. Young people have all the energy, yet no time. Older ones have all the time, but no energy. Anyway, I always tell your mama and his daughter that my eyes yearned the most to see you, maybe for one last time. It has been over eight years that I last saw you. Don't think I am complaining. I know that is what one typifies old age with. I am just trying to recount everything.

I still remember standing inside that hospital room when you were born. I also remember your mummy and papa back then, fighting about the most trivial of issues even when she was in labor. In my heart, I knew that they were not meant for each other. But as a caring Indian mother, all I could do was wish well for her and hoped she could save her marriage. Then, you came into their life.

Initially, things were okay for them and I could see them living a life of compromise for your sake. The naughtier you were while growing up, the busier your mother got. It seemed that incompatibility with your father had become a secondary issue.

Talking about your childhood, we all knew that you are meant for anything but an ordinary life, given your astonishing intelligence and carefree attitude. You were a born maverick and I remember telling your mother once that you will grow up to become a famous artist and do her proud. This was when you failed in a junior class and she couldn't stop crying. Anyway, little did I know then, that the distance between her and your father was growing too, alongside. Your mother is my oldest child and right from her teenage years, she has been the second mother to her siblings. She is very strong inside, seldom sharing her pain or her real emotions with anyone else. I guess you also have this trait. How I wish you stayed with her and not your father after their separation. This is one conversation I had with her too often. She kept saying, 'Abhay will decide what is best for him.' She sacrificed so much and lived through a failed marriage for eighteen years, so that her son would get normal growing up years. And yet, that son chose to desert her, when she needed him the most.

I know you will not agree with me. I won't blame you for it. Again, it is for my emotional and stupid daughter's belief of not sharing her pain with her only son. But yes, Abhay, through this letter, I want you to know that your mother has seen suffering but has never told you or anyone else about it. To date, I remain the only person who knows what she has been through. It speaks volumes of her strength, but a lot about her silliness too. What is the point of hiding your reality? What do you get out of it? I guess every person is a hero, in her own mind.

So, my dear grandson, I want you to fulfill my last wish. It is the last wish of a dying woman. For my sake, make an effort and reach out to your mother. Don't call her, but surprise her or visit her even if only for a few minutes. I have a belief that she will break down and let her emotions out. I am sure you will forgive her. Even if this happens after I am gone, believe me, this will help my soul rest in peace.

Always wishing health and happiness for you and Sujata,
Your loving Nani.

I was choked with emotion. This two page letter and a couple of old pictures of me playing as I sat on her lap were not the only contents of that box that Nani had left behind for me. It also had a broken hairpin which I now remembered tampering with as a child every time I visited her home. I never knew she cared so much so as to preserve it for me.

The letter made me think. What did she mean by Mom going through pain and keeping it to herself? Did she mean the fights my parents had? Given the way my parents were, they probably fought and argued two hundred times more behind my back than they did in front of me. Nani was right there. They had done a good job by protecting me from that ugliness.

The next afternoon, Unnati and Sasha sat next to each other in the car, but did not talk to each other. I lay on the backseat as Sasha drove us out of Goa.

Honestly, I had not expected the previous night to go so well. All I had planned for was to get Sasha caught red-handed at a rave. Using drugs, and that too next to a girl, was pure bonus. With nothing much to do during this ride, I decided to use my time to look through Nani's box. I suddenly felt the pressure of fulfilling her last wish, however difficult it may be for me. Curiosity gripped me. It wasn't that I had decided to reconcile with my mother after reading the letter. But I really wanted to know her side of the story. But then, there was another, more recent event unfolding right before my eyes.

After going back to our resort the previous night, Unnati had cried all night in her room while Sasha fell flat on the bed, overtaken by guilt and the effect of the drugs. It wasn't until late next morning that the both of them came out of their rooms. Sasha started pleading with Unnati for forgiveness.

"Baby, I swear to God, what you saw wasn't true!" he went down on his knees right outside her room. She stood with her hands folded across her chest, and a straight face. Her puffy eyes showed that she had been crying all night.

I stood there and she suddenly turned to me, "Ab, please tell this guy that whatever it was, I don't really care."

"Unns, please, at least let me tell you what happened!" he said, still on the ground.

"Don't you dare call me that! Now move, and let me be," she said in haste and turned to go back to her room.

She stopped and said to me, "Abhay, I can't travel with you guys, especially him, anymore. Sorry."

She slammed the door shut behind her.

I was flabbergasted at her decision. I expected that she'd be mad at him, fight with him and then break up. But this was a drastic step. I banged on her door, forcing her to open it.

"Unnati, open up and listen to me. Can you please let me in and hear me out once?" I asked.

"I can listen to you. But not with him around," she said, pointing at Sasha as she opened the door slightly.

I begged him, "Bhai please!" I said, and he understood.

I went into Unnati's room.

I made her sit down on the sofa and said, "Unnati, you are absolutely right about him. He is an idiot and deserves every bit of punishment you choose for him," I began to brainwash her.

"You are to blame, too. He wasn't alone. You are the smarter one. My parents sent me on this trip because they thought you were mature."

I nodded and admitted that I did get carried away. "You are right, we both got carried away. He shouldn't have; after all, he is committed to you. Anyway, I wasn't taking drugs, I didn't even realize that those girls had those intentions!"

She didn't reply. I continued, "Unnati, listen to me, please. You may choose to call off your relationship with him if you want to, but you shouldn't jeopardize our entire effort. At least think of it as a professional commitment to a movie. You can treat it as a professional engagement. Just tag along for your own career's sake."

She was silent. Finally, she said, "I need time to think. Please leave me alone."

I went out and Sasha grabbed my arm. "What did she say?"

"I don't know. I think she will agree. Even if she does, saving your relationship will be very difficult," I said, secretly enjoying the act of rubbing salt on his wounds.

"Don't say that! Bhai, how did she know we were partying?"

"I don't know, Sasha. Do you want me to ask her that?" I asked, irritated, and went to my room.

❖

That Unnati agreed to come along was given. It was obvious that she would continue to be mad at him. She made it clear in no uncertain terms. "Guys, I am done with whatever happened. It is the past now. From hereon, we are three professionals who happen to know each other and have a past. I have no interest in friendship or anything anymore and I expect the same from you, especially Sashank. If he tries to get too friendly, I will back out."

We nodded. Sasha thought that time would heal the situation. I kept thinking of how she would soon be mine. With those thoughts, we left the beaches of Goa and a part of our souls behind.

We were driving to Mysore at snail's pace, as Sashank was preoccupied with his thoughts. I thought I should volunteer to drive, but decided to try out my luck instead (sorry Nani, you gotta wait).

"Unnati, have you spoken to your mom of late? I am sure she'd be happy to learn about the Bingo Productions development!" I asked her casually and broke into a grin.

"Hmm…," she said. "She was very happy about it."

"Did you tell her about our meeting with Suraj?"

"I told her about what you guys did in Goa."

Sasha slammed the brakes. "What did she say?" he asked, worried.

"She told me to stay away from you and gave me a good lecture on how she had always been wary of you. I never listened to her, I guess that's why I am suffering now."

She looked straight ahead as she spoke. Meanwhile her ex continued frowning. Their break-up was now official with her mother having gotten involved. After a while, Sasha asked me, "Ab, can we switch?" I willingly took charge.

As Sasha slept in the backseat, we navigated through NH-4 to enter Karnataka. I tried initiating a conversation again. "Wow! The weather is changing. I guess we can rest the air conditioner for a while and roll down the windows. What do you say?"

She nodded. Soon, the breeze hit us from both sides. It was an empty road, contrary to my expectations. But, the air was certainly fresher and got cooler as twilight set in. "Look how the weather can change within a few hours. It was so hot till this afternoon and suddenly it's changed! What an analogy to compare our lives with," I commented.

"My life has certainly changed over the last twenty-four hours," Unnati sounded hurt. Sasha was asleep.

I didn't give up easily, I had to make my soft move after all. "It may even be for the better."

Her face turned and our eyes met for a split second. She looked ahead and said, "It is not about your friend, Abhay, I know he is a little clueless. The problem is with me."

"I don't understand."

"I allow others to dominate my mind-space and heart. If you let another person do that to you, you are indirectly giving them the right to hurt you as well. I am done with relationships now." She had all but ripped her heart open. She began crying.

I cajoled her. "Hey, come on, Unns! It's okay, it's not your fault."

I slowed down the car and half-hugged her, feeling quite content with myself. I continued, "It's called love, and is a cocktail of pain, satisfaction, sadness and happiness, all at the same time. Believe me, it's Sasha's fault and bad luck. Don't blame or change yourself for the mistake he made."

I pressed her arm tight while saying that. She settled in a little into my embrace and I enjoyed this little physical intimacy (that's how sick I am!). She freed herself and brushed her tears away while throwing her head back. After a while, she asked me, "What did your Nani write in the letter?"

"I can't tell you everything now, but I promise I will. She left me some pictures from my childhood. They are in the dashboard."

She smiled and opened it quickly to grab the brown envelope of pictures. It had my Nani and me in black and white. I looked like an overfed baby.

Her infectious laughter was back. "Did you eat all the food back then?" Her eyes grew sad again at the mere thought of the sleeping giant in the backseat. I found a strange sense of satisfaction in her reactions.

I lightened the mood, "I was born underweight and was pretty thin. Then I was often bullied by other kids of my age. At home, they fed me these packaged foods as a four-year-old so that I could gain weight. It did wonders, so yes I was an overfed Cerelac baby."

She couldn't stop laughing. I continued, "What? Hey it's not that I am still fat. Why are you laughing? Don't you go on a diet and eat sprouts or *gheeya-tori-tinde* or other inedible stuff when you have to lose weight? Then what's wrong with doing the opposite to gain?"

She had her hands over her eyes, as she laughed.

I continued joking, coming up with silly one-liners. She laughed at all of them. We continued our conversation till late in the night when we finally halted at a little roadside inn near Bhadravati Taluka. Though the fan didn't work and the mattress underneath was thinner than a newspaper, I slept very well that night.

❖

Mysore was primarily a food destination more than anything else. As the gateway to South India for our trip, it is also the place where idli, dosa and sambhar are dished out aplenty. The Maharaja Palace, the Chamundi Temple and the Zoological Gardens are a must-see on every visitor's list, but we had come for food.

"What do we tell everyone when we go back? That we didn't look around the city where South Indian food is found?" Sasha had asked me when we had made our initial list of places to visit.

"Dosa is eaten everywhere in Karnataka. If you really want to go to its place of origin, we should go to Udupi," I had said.

He was adamant about Mysore. He also pressured me by dropping the names of some eateries that were famous for their dosas along with the city's jewel, the Maharaja Palace, which receives the second highest number of visitors in India after the Taj Mahal. So there we were, on our first day in Mysore, looking the least enthusiastic as a group, except for its captain.

"Come on guys! Perk up a little! We are here for work, remember?" I said. We had stopped for lunch at a local joint.

A waiter came up to us lazily and said, "Sir, order maadi..." and continued to say something in his local language. I looked at him blankly.

"No English?" Unnati asked. He shook his head.

"Hindi?" Same answer.

"Welcome to South India!" I told my friends and quickly took my camera and focused on him. He became conscious, smiled and ran away. Shortly, the owner of the restaurant appeared with a white silk shawl along his shoulders and a lungi that could unfold any moment.

"Sir, no Hindi, no English. Order?"

Sasha was excited.

"Sir, we are very hungry very!" he said, rubbing his own, and then my stomach. The owner showed him the menu again, which was in Kannada.

"Sir, bring your best food. Any. Three portions. No. Four. Best. With sambar, rasam and chutney!" Sasha said.

Perhaps a foodie knew how to communicate effectively. The owner miraculously understood him and showed him a thumbs-up sign. Soon, there were four huge thalis filled with dosas, idlis, sambar, some rice and a variety of curries. We ate hungrily.

By evening, we knew that including Mysore was a good decision. The Maharaja Amba Palace was one of the most beautiful we had seen in our lives. It was well lit and resembled a beautiful, decked-up Indian bride in full glory. Under the night sky, Unnati offered a review while dressed in local attire, standing right outside the main gate. We rested the next day as we decided to stay indoors and do some editing. Sasha went out to the local market to try more food. Unnati stayed in her room, having taken the idea of being professional a little too seriously. I tried talking her out of it, but in vain. The two days at Mysore had food written all over them. Both my friends were coping well with their break up and Sasha was more subdued than I expected.

It was a positive sign to the little goodness left in me. I wanted them to be away from each other, but I wanted my friend to cheer up as well. The way he held up made it appear that at least that part of my plan had worked well enough. As Unnati said, life can take you from a secure place to being messed up with the snap of a finger. I didn't know that the volcano inside him was nearing eruption.

Love can make
you do crazy things

It felt a little stupid to take my selfie without them against a sign-board that said 'Mysore.' We were set to drive out the next day. Unnati refused to be clicked in a picture with Sasha. He claimed that he was too hurt at her comment to be ready to pose. Not able to stand their tantrums, I decided to do it alone, no matter how stupid it would look.

Kanyakumari, our country's southernmost tip and our next destination, was a day's drive. We had begun feeling trapped in the car. The human mind can create illusions in layers, as the actors in famous Hollywood movie *Inception* convincingly portrayed. Our minds started believing that there was one life we were living and another that we lived out of this car. Every now and then, we lived in our 'other life,' but soon, it was back-to-life in the car. My dreams were more about this cage-hole than about Unnati now.

I told my friends that we had to have an extra day's stop over at Kanyakumari as opposed to the original plan of staying for a couple of nights. It wasn't only the 600 kilometer odd drive from every city that was taking its toll, but it was more of mental exhaustion. And their fight added to it.

Unnati had come to terms with life without Sasha. The moment we checked into our hotel at Kanyakumari, she told me,

"I don't want to sit inside any longer. Please let me know when you head out tomorrow morning."

That night, I just couldn't sleep. One, because of yet another tiring day on the road. Two, because Sasha had ordered huge portions of Chettinad Chicken and liquor through room service.

"Are you nuts, Sasha? It's 11:00 p.m. and not a good time to drink. Why don't you get some sleep and let me sleep as well?" I raised my voice at him.

He didn't bother and made a peg for himself. I jerked my head in disapproval and went to take a shower. When I stepped out of the bathroom, from the look of the little service table, I realized that he was well drunk. I taunted him again. "Last time you got drunk, you got into big trouble. What do you have in mind now?"

He looked at me with red eyes. I was suddenly scared.

He said, "You want to see what I am up to? Wait and watch!"

He picked up the landline and called Unnati's phone in her room. After a few rings, she answered.

Sasha said, "You will not see me, I know. But what is the harm if you speak to me on the phone? Just listen to what I have to say. Suddenly, because of one episode, have I become bad or no longer trustworthy? I have done crazier stuff before, haven't I?"

I didn't get to hear what she said, but I knew where this was heading. After a pause, Sasha said, "So what if I was inhaling that drug? Could you not see how drunk I was? Do you think I was in my complete senses and did it on purpose?" his voice was getting louder now. I knew it was heading towards a bad apology.

He stood up and almost half-shouted, "What do you mean I was kissing that girl? Is kissing someone a crime when you are sloshed and have no clue what's happening? You are being unreasonable here, Unns! Don't tell me that you haven't kissed anyone before meeting me! You bit…" he couldn't even finish.

I think she had slammed the phone down. In less than a minute, there was a knock on our door. I opened it to find her standing there.

"I knew that he was a pig and wouldn't let me complete this trip in peace. Did I not tell you this? I have had enough of his crap now, Ab. I am going to Delhi tomorrow by myself, thank you for a wonderful tour Mr. Producer!" She turned around and stormed off.

I turned to Sasha. "Bhai, what is this?" He just showed me his middle finger in response. I felt like a middleman being thwarted both by my supplier and my customer here.

"Go to hell, both of you!" I yelled and went inside the washroom again.

A shrilling loud screech made me run back outside, "Sasha!" I shouted on at the top of my voice.

He had broken his empty liquor bottle on the table and gripped a thick piece of glass in his right palm, ready to cut his other hand with it. His right palm was already bleeding.

"What the fuck are you doing?" I jumped like a superhero from the bathroom door onto the sofa and grabbed his wrist tightly to stop him from hurting himself. He reacted crazily and sank his teeth into my hand. I yelped in pain, but kept my grip intact. When he realized that I was not going to give up, he threw the glass on the floor and started crying. If anyone had entered our room at that moment, they'd probably think that we had a big fight. My hand hurt from his bite, but I was not going to give up. I quickly brushed the bigger pieces of glass under the bed, lest he got tempted to pick one up again.

"Sasha, get a grip on yourself, buddy. It's okay," I said lightly, handing him a glass of water.

He took the glass. "Nothing will be alright. I have seen enough and I know Unnati will go back tomorrow and chuck me out of her life forever. It's all over. My life's over, too!" He howled. It's tough to see a man cry, however feeble he may be.

"Even if that happens, is that the end of the world? I mean, is she the only girl around? You will find someone better than her..." I said, sharing what I really wanted for him in my grand scheme of things. As a reaction, though, he got up and picked up the broken bottle from the table. I quickly pulled it out of his hand.

"Give me that bottle, Ab. You know that I can't live without Unnati. Give me that bottle now!"

In my heart, I was being stabbed by hundreds of daggers as Sasha cried, "She is the only girl I have ever been with or known. How can you even think that I can find someone else? Don't you remember how I bored you to death with stories about her? Don't you remember how I bunked college on her birthday and got caught and missed my final semester? Don't you remember how I gave up my crazy work-ideas so that her parents found my business a respectable career choice? Ab, she is my breath and the only reason for me to live. You know everything. You know me more than myself. You always used to say that. How can you even suggest that I forget her and move on!"

He kept crying after that. He was right. How could I ever forget all these incidents? I kept sitting on that floor, blowing warm air on my right hand that Sasha had wounded mercilessly a few minutes ago. However, it was nothing compared to the storm that I had brought into his life. He was my friend, companion and brother. The only person in this world who loved me, unconditionally, and I could trust in my sleep. And what had I done to him? I had gotten infatuated with my best buddy's girl and then ruined their relationship in the hope of getting hitched to her? I had to put a stop to this! The devil was back in my mind here – *'So what Ab, this was bound to happen. Someone's relationship gets broken so they create melodrama, big deal.'*

'This is not a joke, he could have died.'

'You think he'd have actually killed himself. Come on! It's only alcohol making him do silly things. And anyway, Unnati can be yours only after she moves away from him…that's how life works.'

'Yeah? Even if she comes to me, what will I tell Sasha? That you two broke up so I hooked with her? Would he not be hurt and hate me then?'

'Don't get into this please-all game. You love her so you get her, rule

of the jungle. if he was man enough, he could have protected his relationship. Love vs friendship, you chose love!'

'I was a fool that I chose this. This is not love, this is pure jealousy. How can I spoil two people's beautiful relationship, with 1 of them being more than my best friend? And then it is not even guaranteed that Unnati will come to me after all this. But it is certain that Sasha wont live a day without her.'

'Whatever! I don't think you should do anything stupid especially now that the hard part is over. Just give them some time and both will be fine,' the devil argued one last time.

'I don't think I will ever be able to live in peace if I separate them and even win over her later. Also I can't do this to Sasha, my only friend Not anymore.'

I got up and walked up to him. With wet eyes, I embraced him hard. He clearly needed this hug as he tightened his grip and wept even more. After letting him shed more tears, I pulled back and told him, "It is my fault that you two are in this spot. I will make sure that I fix things."

He didn't understand anything, but kept looking into my eyes. For the first time in weeks, mine returned his gaze with genuine love and assurance.

The next morning, Unnati didn't come out of her room, as expected. Sasha and I woke up with severe headaches, thanks to our bromance and drinks the previous night. However, I felt light and refreshed as the devil had been kicked out of my system. I was back to being the Abhay I was, the Abhay who only cared for his friends and focused on making this road trip a rocking success. Yes, there was pain, as I wasn't over her completely. But I knew how wrong I had been.

We took an Aspirin each and went to the hotel's breakfast buffet to grab a bite. After a while, Unnati walked into the restaurant. From a distance, she still looked a desirable diva to me. But that impulse was replaced timely by the urge to reunite my friends. She served herself some food and went to a different table. Sasha and I looked at each other, but I signaled to him to continue eating. I then picked up my plate and walked up to Unnati. She continued staring down her plate as I sat opposite her.

"So what's the plan, when do you leave?"

I guess she was surprised at my defiance that I didn't try to reason with her or ask her to stay. "Unfortunately, there is no flight today."

I smiled but remained silent. Probably she got it through her sixth sense as she added, "But there is a flight tomorrow morning, from Thiruvananthapuram. I will take a taxi from the hotel to the airport early tomorrow."

"So, you have decided."

"Yes!"

"Okay, in that case, I won't stop you," I said, "But I must tell you that the road trip will be finished as planned and the movie will be made, too. I will probably be the voice. Or Sasha will take over. Or maybe I will hire a voice-over artist, but it will surely be finished. And released too."

"Good for you!"

She was blunt, and thumped her hands hard on the table, while poking her face out at me.

"Yep baby, good it is! It is good, indeed."

"Why do you make it sound as if I am being the hurdle in your plans? Why don't you go ahead and say all this to him?"

"Because he is not the one withdrawing. It is you. Yes, you guys had a big fight, but the relationship was made of two people, not one. Here, you are acting as if only you got hurt and you are the poor one, the...the... victim. And oh cry for me. He is not killing the trip, you are!" I remained firm in my words.

"I don't care anymore. I am going."

"I won' t stop you either." I made a move to get up.

Before I left, I added, "By the way, you are still stuck here for another day for no fault of your own. We are going to Vivekananda

Rock, the endpoint of India, this afternoon. If you want you can join us, not as a friend or a crewmember, but as a fellow tourist. You've come this far, I thought you'd might as well see it. You may not want to come with him but I know he won't mind if you came."

I got up and went back to my table without waiting for a reaction. Sasha asked me what had happened but I refused to say anything and finished breakfast. Later that morning, Unnati joined us, wearing shorts and carrying a small backpack. Nobody said anything to each other. Soon, we drove to the beach.

The beach was flooded with men and women selling small flower garlands, touristy knick-knacks and idli-sambar. We boarded an overcrowded ferry to take us to Vivekananda Rock. The entire journey hung precariously between life and death, because (a) There was no space and even a tennis ball dropped anywhere in that ferry could have sunk it, and (b) I had told Sasha that this would be the only private time he could get with Unnati and he had to make it count. Luckily for him, the South Indian tourists around us didn't seem to know a word of our lingo. Sasha sat beside me. Unnati was to my left. He got up and said, "Unnati, can I talk to you, please?"

She got up looking for another place to sit. He started mock crying. Everyone looked at him – it seemed a giant was weeping like a newborn and it was too funny a sight to miss.

With Sasha's histrionics, our ferry began to shake. The operator shouted at him, saying something that we couldn't understand. Oblivious to the instructions, Sasha started moving. The boat tilted and before we could think of anything, Unnati who was on the edge, fell into the water.

"Go after her, you idiot!" I shouted at him and pushed him in as well. Luckily, they both knew how to swim. Sasha put up enough of a show to make everyone in our boat believe that he had actually saved her, as everyone threw their arms out and pulled them back.

Once back on the shore, Unnati looked at Sasha, angrily. "I could have drowned because of you! Please, I beg to be forgiven. It's my mistake that I got into a relationship with you. Can you please let me live my life? After hurting me emotionally, today you hurt me physically as well."

Sasha stood with a bowed head and mustered just enough courage to say, "Please, one last time?"

In response, she walked in the other direction, towards the memorial. I stood like a dummy, knowing of my friend's inability to stitch a good apology. I owed them both one myself.

"Guys, Unns, wait a second. I have to tell you both something," I said.

"Please, Abhay!" she said, dropping her shoulders, and looking jaded. "I beg you too. I seriously have no energy left."

"Trust me, Unnati, you want to hear this. The real reason for all this is not him, it's me. I was the one who started it."

"Yeah I know."

"You do?"

"Yeah. You secretly love me and that's why you caused our break up, right? Stop living for your friend, Abhay!"

"No! But that's the truth. I forced him or rather induced him to ditch you, go to this party secretly and…"

She cut me short. "Blah blah blah! Whatever! I am still not interested. You could have come up with something better." She turned around and walked away.

Sasha patted me on my shoulder. "Bhai, you love me so much that you can lie to this extent? Come on, give me a hug. I promise you, I will never try to commit suicide again. What if I don't have her, I have you at least!" He threw his arms around me.

"Unbelievable!" I exclaimed hugging him. So now the devious plan, the reality behind their grand break up was a mere lie to the world! She was not going to believe the real version. Forget her, even this potato wasn't going to buy it.

"Sasha, enough drama. Now if you have to win your girl back, you have to do something really filmy, man. These apologies, these stories aren't working." I told him as we walked towards the queue to enter memorial's main area.

"She is right, you can come up with something better," he said sarcastically.

"Look around you, there is the sea and a nice breeze blowing. What a romantic setting."

"Warm," he added.

"Yeah, a warm and serene breeze. And then there is this historical monument where Vivekananda sat before he embarked on his journey. It is a symbol of love – a place where all new and divine journeys start from."

"I don't understand."

"Propose to her! Ask her to marry you. Right here, right now."

"What? Are you nuts? She is not interested in talking to me and you are asking me to propose to her?"

"Why not? She wants to settle down. She wants a man who will be committed to her till eternity. She wants that sense of security. She confessed to me once, twice to be fair, that she is looking for that kind of commitment from you. And you, fucker, you almost slashed your wrist for her! Isn't that proof that you need her to be with you?" I reasoned with him.

"Yeah, but this is not the time. She will laugh at me for even making an attempt at this juncture of our relationship."

"Even better! Actually, that's what I want. Shock her! Why did she get mad at you? You broke her trust, right? Come up with some good lines about commitment and propose to her this evening."

He said he needed time to think. I had asked my best friend to propose marriage to the girl I was infatuated with. But strangely, it didn't feel as painful as I had thought it would. After an hour of wandering about, Sasha came to me and said, "Ab, I have a plan. Come with me. Don't ask, just follow and play along."

I had become a criminal, a prankster, a ghost-hunter and even a jealous lover in the last few days. But I never thought I would become a dacoit, who would force an administrative staff member with a knife and a fake threat so that my buddy could propose to his girlfriend. But there I was, standing behind the Vivekananda

Rock Memorial where there was only one guy. He was now at my mercy, or, as I told him, my gang surrounding the memorial would open fire.

I forcefully took the mic from him and announced, "Ladies and gentlemen. Today, we have a special service and an educational film to be screened on the life of Shree Vivekananda. I request everyone to move to our new amphitheater and patiently sit down. The movie will begin shortly."

I signaled a thumbs-up to Sasha, who rushed to make arrangements. The guy under my threat seemed confused, but I remained stern. Meanwhile, in the amphitheater, around five hundred people had assembled. I could see from the CCTV cameras in the greenroom that I was in that Unnati had also found a seat. I saw all the action on multiple screens, and was waiting for Sasha to appear. Then the movie started. It played out initial credits of Bingo Productions and I saw Unnati getting interested. I asked the guy to zoom one of the cameras on her while another monitor showed me the movie.

I appeared on the amphitheater's screen in a close-up and did a little jig and said pointing my finger, "This one is for you, Unnati!" and disappeared.

Some of the rushes from our trip appeared on the screen. Randomly. Some shots where both Sasha and Unnati were laughing, or holding hands. Of her sitting in front of an aged-audience in a desert-camp and reciting her love story, Sasha hugging her and screaming in delight after our deal with the Bingo Productions team, and so on.

After a minute of these random videos, Sasha's voice could be heard,

"Every minute of my life, I have loved and only loved you. I am fat and ugly while you are beautiful, but we have always made a good pair. People have been jealous of us and you know it too. Every morning when I wake up, the first thought that comes to my mind is how I can make this day special for you. Yes, it comes before I think about what to eat for breakfast."

The audience laughed and could sense a real proposal going on here, but nobody seemed to mind.

Meanwhile, Unnati was clearly in shock, with her hands on her cheeks. She could deny talking to him, but she couldn't get away from this without watching the whole video.

His voice continued, "I know I hurt you, again and again and again. And you forgive me each time. But this time I went too far. To your bad luck, you've got a silly boyfriend. To ensure that you teach me a lesson for my stupidity, it's important for us to stay together, isn't it?

"I also know that it is inappropriate because our family isn't here. But Unnati, no Unns, I thought it's important to ask you first. "It is a little old-fashioned and extremely far-reaching of me to ask when you are upset with me, but Unnati Bhatia, will you marry me? I deserve this as a chance to make up for the last mistake of mine. And also the thousands of mistakes I am going to make. But I know you love me with all my flaws and I want to express my gratitude for it. Please say yes and I promise I will take good care of you in sickness, in old age and in bad times."

I could see on the monitor that Unnati's eyes were wet.

And then our EcoSport appeared on-screen. Sasha wearing dark sunglasses was driving and stopped it with a jerk in macho style. He stepped down and started running towards the screen. The movie stopped and lights were back on. I mentally patted myself for my shooting and presentation skills.

Unnati was both happy and surprised to see him standing in front of her in person.

Sasha bent down on his knees in front of Unnati and the crowd in that amphitheater and asked her, "Will you marry me, Unnati?"

Everyone started clapping, including the person in that backroom. I clapped the hardest though, and saw her crying and just nodding a yes. My friend had done it. He not only won her heart back and proposed, but had done it in a grand style! Something I never expected him to. But love can make you do crazy things.

Hyderabadi
Food Jockeys

We were back in the hotel. Unnati couldn't stop gushing with excitement as she came to terms with the anticipation of marriage and being proposed to in an enviable style. I was right about Unnati. She just couldn't resist the temptation of getting married, and was already behaving like a newly-wed bride. The big fight had brought her a bigger prize.

I took it all with a pinch of salt; I knew I would have been happier if I was in Sasha's place. But it didn't matter. It was their day and their love story to begin with.

I reconciled to the fact and was determined to be happy for my friend instead.

I kept teasing them through the remainder of our stay at Kanyakumari. Unnati put forth her modesty-card. Sashank was subdued and happy to be back with her more than anything else. They had lunch together in privacy and asked me to mind my own business for the rest of the afternoon. It was all in good spirit, and for once, life seemed so beautiful and uncluttered. I felt a new zeal to complete this journey, and to go back to our producers to release the movie with a probable appearance in the India Book of Records for the maximum number of kilometers covered on an Indian road trip for three movie-makers.

The following day, we bid goodbye to Kanyakumari, which was an unforgettable destination in their life story. We clicked a selfie with number 14 outside our hotel.

I teased them, saying, "When your grandchildren celebrate your fiftieth wedding anniversary, show them this picture and tell them this is where it all started. I am sure they'll ask you Unnati, why you didn't choose this better looking guy over Dadaji!" I got two fingers as horns in my selfie as a result.

Our next destination was Rameshwaram, a holy city in Tamil Nadu, and a short distance away from Kanyakumari. We had included Rameshwaram in our itinerary to visit the Ram Setu Bridge. According to Hindu mythology, Lord Rama got this thirty kilometer bridge made by monkeys who threw stones in the water so that he and his army of monkeys could cross and go to Lanka and rescue his kidnapped wife. We reached Rameshwaram by the evening and rested in a small lodge. This time we decided to do something unique. We wanted to explore this holy city like tourists and got a guide. This way, at least the atheist in me could differentiate between this one and the temples we had seen so far. To me, they all looked the same.

Our guide for this one day tour, Mr Ramanna, was a young friendly chap. He looked more like a body builder than a guide. He had the spirit of a cruel sports coach as he made us wake up at 5:00 a.m. and took us through a twenty-two-well bath ritual at the Ramnathswami Temple.

He told us during the second dip, "Lord Rama did this to wash off his sins for having killed the Rakshasa dynasty. Therefore, it is believed that all our sins can be done away with if one successfully completes this ritual."

Unnati remarked, "This is for you then, Sasha and Ab. You guys can be absolved of your Goan encounter!"

After a while, maybe our ninth or tenth dip, I wondered if doing away with one's sins was so easy, why didn't I make it an annual visit?

The feeling of an early morning darshan, the holy ambience around the bath ritual and the soothing architecture of that temple got to me. I felt like I was in a different world once it had gotten over. We followed it with many more temple visits and by the evening, we felt like veterans on temple tours.

"A day spent well! I don't know if it looks beautiful on your television screens, but I can bet nothing can match the splendor and godly feeling that you get while standing in Rameshwaram. Even the Ram Setu Bridge is not visible to the naked eye, but somehow makes its presence felt if you stand here and stare in its direction for a while. The world may say it's a myth or whatever, but you can feel it and absorb it at a spiritual level and certainly go back with a redefined soul," Unnati said, as we shot the video on the last day.

We clapped at her impromptu dialogue delivery, straight from the heart. "If Rameshwaram tourism grows next year, you deserve a fat paycheque, Unns!" I complimented her

❖

Leaving Rameshwaram was an adventure in itself. We had completed the north to south journey. This earmarked our return path. It gave us a special sense of achievement. We had been on the road for forty-eight days and were tired. But the recent string of events, and particularly Sasha and Unnati's engagement, had infused a renewed sense of excitement in us. Reaching our next stop was to be the longest drive in this tour and bisected three states. We were going to Hyderabad, embarking on a drive that would last two days. We had to pass through Tamil Nadu, cross Andhra Pradesh and then finally reach India's newest state, Telangana.

"Our school teachers would be so proud of you!" I poked at Sasha as he discussed the route map.

"As if you scored well. You barely passed," he shot back.

We navigated on NH-7 and decided that this voyage would be our last one with a round of authentic sambhar and idlis. Once in Hyderabad, we were not going to go anywhere near it.

"Hyderabad promises a Nawabi feast!" quipped Sasha as we settled down for lunch at a highway restaurant, again with a loud billboard promising the best idlis in Tamil Nadu – Murugan Idli Shop.

"Chottu, do you make dal, err, lentil curry?" I asked a young server.

"Sir, there is a Punjabi dhaba in the city. Why bother coming to Madurai if you don't try our special food?" he said candidly, in Hindi, for a change. We were delighted. It was tough to find a Hindi-speaking boy in these south cities.

"We are done with your idli-sambhar! Can you ask the chef to make something different for us?" Unnati asked.

"Wait, Fair and Lovely ma'am! I will personally get some special items for you!" he announced and ran back inside. We laughed at his words. Soon, he brought a thambi, or brother in local lingo, with him. He laid out an extravagant spread and named the dishes as he placed them before us. "Methu vadai, paniyaram, chilly bajji, uthaappam, ghee rava dosa, lemon rice, tomato rice and lastly, my favorite, our special thali!" he announced. The food looked good and we were hungry so we dived in without further invitation.

"Delicious!" Sasha said, and asked for more. The boy gladly obliged and served him. I initiated a friendly chat with him, "How much do you get? As a salary, if you don't mind."

"Two thousand rupees, sir."

"Is that it? How do you manage? Do you go to school?"

"I get a good salary, sir. The guy who served you gets 1,500 rupees. I take orders, so I get more," he said, proudly.

We all looked at each other. Unnati asked, "What about your chef?"

"Not sure. Around 3,500 rupees, I think. He makes the best South Indian food here."

Sasha, who was done eating, said, "I can vouch for that. It was our best meal indeed. Here, young boy, get the bill! God bless you and your chef for keeping my faith in your cuisine alive."

He gave him fifty rupees and the boy ran inside gleefully.

Soon, we were on our way again when Sasha said, "See? This is the problem with this country. We ate at so many expensive places across Kerala, Karnataka and Tamil Nadu, but this was by far the best sambar we had. And these guys make a pittance selling it."

For once we nodded at his studious observation. It was well past evening as we drove. Our rule of not driving after sunset had been discarded. Sasha volunteered to drive through the night if Unnati agreed to keep him engaged with her interesting talk. That bastard had finally picked romantic language. I was lying in the backseat with closed eyes and listened to them.

"Poochie, what do you think would be a good date for our wedding?" she asked.

"Do you know it's been ages since you last called me Poochie? I love it when you do that!"

She giggled. "You've learned and improved. Ab was right."

"Unns, he has done so much for me. I wish I could find him a partner as good as you. It will be so much fun, then."

"We must do it for him when we go back. I want you to push him to reconcile with his family. We have one life, after all. Till he lets it go, he won't really find inner peace," she said. I listened to them and felt grateful.

"Yeah, I will. Let me share a secret," Sasha told her while checking on me in the rear-view mirror. "I read his Nani's letter. It was in the car's dashboard. I know what needs to be done."

Bastard, I thought, but I didn't want to give it away, so I remained still.

"You are more wicked than you look! What did the letter say?" asked Unnati so conveniently. She forgot her high morals, et al, just like that, and now wanted the gossip.

"I didn't understand all of it, but I guess his Nani wants him to speak to his mother once, for her sake. I agree with her, actually. Ab is arrogant when it comes to making the first move."

"Where did you read it, by the way?" she asked him.

"In Goa. When we went to the party, he went out to get some drinks."

"Don't remind me of that incident. Thank god for the helpful manager. Otherwise I would have never found you out!" Unnati said, faking some leftover anger.

"By the way, how did that manager know we went for this party? It was a very discreet thing."

My heart stopped for a second.

Unnati said, "I didn't bother to ask. All he said was that all the young guys and girls staying at the hotel were there. He arranged for a taxi for me and didn't ask for money either!"

"That's odd. As far as I remember, there was no one from our hotel there," he wondered.

"How would you know all the people?"

"Because Abhay and I had lazed around the pool long enough to notice the good looking birds staying there. "

Unnati added to suspicion, "Yeah… at that time I didn't think about this, but how did the manager know exactly where you were? I hardly gave him any details except your room number."

They were silent for a while, and looked at each other. Sasha brought out his phone and checked his log records.

"I was probably too drunk to notice, but Ab wasn't," he said.

Suddenly, they looked at each other and said in unison, "You think? Ab?"

There was utter silence in the car for a while. My heart was skipping its beats so frequently that I could have suffered a mild attack had Sasha not spoken up.

"No. He is my best friend and won't do anything of this sort to me. I will ask him directly, rather than make presumptions."

Unnati was quiet. Maybe refraining from saying anything.

My respect for him increased a hundred notches. He was a friend worth dying for.

❖

We reached Hyderabad after two days of tiring drive. Maybe it was this drive or the toll of the entire journey that made my back, legs, hands and toes hurt like hell. For a change, it wasn't Sasha and Unnati complaining about our grueling schedule. I told my friends that we'd rather spend an extra day in Hyderabad than drive out in two days because we had a long distance to cover from there onwards.

Hyderabad was home to the Telugu Film Industry. And it was the second-highest place of business (after Mumbai) for Bingo Productions. It brought some welcomed benefits. Firstly, a mini-crew escorted us right from their office where we were to report, to our hotel. We felt like stars to be honest, even though the onlookers had no idea what was happening as a procession of cars went along with us. Secondly, they parked us at Falaknuma Palace – one of the most opulent hotels of our country!

It was a heritage property, right from the days of the Nizams and their begums, and improvised upon by European architectural influence. I could have done an entire shoot on the hotel and its history itself! We could not contain our happiness when one of the crew members bid us goodbye and said, "Miss Tanya from Mumbai was all praises for your concept and your movie. I hope it does well and we get to dub it into Telugu as well for our audiences later. Good luck and give me a buzz if you need anything during your stay in our city."

It brought additional pressure, though we didn't complain. To explore this place, we decided on a slightly different approach than what we had done so far. We expressed our interest in recording their city to a social club that Sasha found online called Hyderabad Food Jockeys. This group of twelve had an amazing passion for their food, and was a self-proclaimed group of lovers, critics and reviewers of Nawabi cuisine. When Sasha emailed them about our trip and our visit to their city, their chief, Sandeep, gladly agreed to not only show us their food hubs, but also accompany us on a cultural and explorative sightseeing tour.

"Hello Sandeep, it's Sasha here!" He called him when our excitement had settled down and we'd ordered half of the poolside menu, creating a big hole in Bingo's pocket.

"Sasha? Who?"

"Sorry…Sashank. I sent you an email from Delhi, a month or so back, remember? For our trip in Hyderabad?" He frowned as he tried to remind him. It was the only thing I had left solely on him to arrange.

Thankfully Sandeep remembered, "Oh yes yes, Sashank ji! I remember, of course. Sorry you said Sasha first so I didn't get you. Anyway, sorry, glad that you are here already. My group is very excited about meeting you guys. We can start tonight. I will pick you up at 7:00 p.m. Do let me know where you are staying."

"No problem. We are at the Taj Falaknuma. Seven is fine. See you, and thanks!" Sasha hung up and told us the plan.

HFJ, the acronym the group used, turned out to be a fun bunch, indeed. Though they were all at least four or five years younger to us, they represented the true cosmopolitan and 21st century Indian spirit of slogging hard in the IT sector in the daytime and heading out for gratification in the evenings. Its founder, Sandeep, was a slightly younger version of Sasha. For a second, I was shocked to see him and then exclaimed, "Here is how you'll look like in the future, buddy!" and pointed at Sasha.

Their group had an equal number of boys and girls and they immediately made us a part of their group. Even before we could raid our first food destination, harmless jokes about Unnati and Sasha's affair or about me being single started. We felt so much at home with them.

Over the next couple of days, they showed us their city from the eyes of a Hyderabadi. We shared light moments, and managed to have those fun moments captured on our camera for our movie. It made the segment look like a rowdy trip. We visited the Charminar,walked around the NTR Gardens, behaved like hooligans and took over all the go-karts for a while at Runway-9, and gave our country a euphoric brand name with our behavior at Ramoji Filmcity. It was all in healthy spirit, nevertheless, looking back, we were not proud of ourselves.

The best part about being with this group was the food. After forty days of cross-country cuisines, we proudly called ourselves food connoisseurs. But they broke our myth in the first meal itself. Our appetizers were boti-boti kebab, magahz masala and tunday kebabi.

"We come from up north. Tunday Kebabi is a Lucknowi dish and we've had plenty of it. Order some Nizami special!" Sasha said.

The waiter seemed miffed and said, "Sir, whatever they may tell you, Tunday Kebabi is a Hyderabadi dish. Haji Murad Ali, the dish's creator belonged to Hyderabad!" and he went to his kitchen. How does one counter that argument? Our group laughed and followed it up with folklore and stories about each of the dishes associated with their cuisine. We learnt about diffferent biryani styles that included dum pukht, qabooli, kachhe gosht ki biryani and even Hyderabadi khichdi. These guys turned out to be really passionate about their food. We reserved our bragging rights for later.

"Okay, your food may be spicy, and perhaps spicier with the mirchi ka salan that you use as curry for all biryanis. But I bet I can eat more portions of biryani than any of you!" Sasha said, as we settled at Paradise Biryani. This place had more Google hits than any other place serving biryani throughout India and we were glad to be there for our last dinner at Hyderabad. Their group, now having sized us up, laughed. It was casual banter, but Sandeep took it seriously.

"You still haven't seen the real me, Sasha Bhai. Your name may be more powerful, but trust me, my buttocks can carry more shit than any other."

"Yuck!" the girls remarked and went off to sit at the largest table available in an already crowded dining area away from us.

"Good one Sandeep, though it's a pity you need it so often. My stomach doesn't let anything pass there so easily at all," Sasha quipped back.

"This is getting serious! So it's Hyderabadi butt versus Delhi's tummy!" someone said and everyone laughed.

"Okay, here is the deal then, Sasha bhai. You eat more biryani than me and I will foot the entire bill. If you can't, you pay for us all. And also admit that Hyderabadis have more capacity than you!" I picked up my camera and positioned it to record the upcoming battle. Someone pricked Sasha. "Come on, Sandeep, he is older. Our digestive system tends to get weaker with age. It is not a fair battle."

Age, food intake capacity and a challenge! It was too much for Sasha to hear. Within minutes, they sat facing each other. Both had a huge plate in front of them. It was a portion meant for three or four people, called Paradise Special Supreme Biryani along with a large bowl of mirchi ka salan. We had surrounded them, rejoicing the good fortune since the loser of the bet had to settle the bill. Within fifteen minutes or so, their platters were on the verge of getting empty and the cheering got louder. By now, the entire restaurant knew some sort of a weird contest was going on here. Some shouted cheers and slogans from their seats. It virtually looked like an IPL match between Delhi and Hyderabad, and home-team clearly outnumbered their opponents.

I was shocked at their capacities! Once their plates were empty, they looked at each other in unison. Neither was willing to give up and signaled for more biryani. This went on for an hour, with occasional breaks for water, toilet or quick walks. It was good fun for the rest of us, though, and we all agreed that it was very difficult to pick a clear winner. It was during their third serving, when Sandeep finally had to stop. Sasha continued to eat. By the look of their plates, it was getting clear that he would emerge as the winner and it seemed that Sandeep would have had to pay a bill that exceeded 15,000 rupees!

"It's not fair. You went to the toilet almost thrice," Sandeep complained.

"Don't talk like a loser, dude. I have clearly eaten more than you. This race was about who eats more and not about who discharges less!" Sasha said, as finally he stopped eating.

I added, "Besides, your world famous buttocks were supposed to carry more, no?" Sasha hi-fived me.

Sandeep turned out to be a sore loser. "No! When you are competing on who can eat more, relieving yourself is like an extra lifeline. It's not a fair move at all!" His mates, or rather, his minions, shrugged in support.

"Easy dude! It's okay! We won't let the secret out when we go back. But for now, admit that you lost," said Sasha.

But Sandeep was defiant. He kept arguing even though he needed a bed to lie down rather than to get into an unnecessary fight. He said, "If you have to cheat and win, why compete, yaar? Next time think ten times before entering a food challenge. I personally brought you to the best of places and this is what you give me in return? Is this your sportsman spirit? Rotten fellow you are!"

I couldn't make sense of his argument from there on. And then, I realized that it was all about his resistance to settle the bill.

So I said, "Hey Sandeep. It's okay buddy. You've been such a nice host. Forget this stupid bet and let me handle the bill. Let's just say it was our treat."

"Do you think I don't want to pay this? How cheap of you to say that!"

This guy had no logic or sanity left as he banged the table hard while saying so.

"Oye, calm down!" Sasha tried.

"How dare you talk to Sandeep like that?" This time it was a girl who spoke on his behalf. I thought Sandeep and she were together. It's amazing how chics fall for potato-like guys in real life. Anyway, that was not important here.

Unnati chipped in and said, "Mind your own business!" Soon, everyone was arguing with everyone else and from nowhere, a bowl of salan was thrown at Sasha. He erupted like a volcano at this point. He picked up a dish full of curry, threw it on Sandeep's head. Sandeep looked down at himself in disbelief, and then at his groupies. His friends jumped on us. Before the blink of an eye, we ran out of the restaurant. There was a lot of yelling behind us, but we kept running. We sprinted through the narrow lanes of Hyderabad and had no idea of our whereabouts, but didn't stop to look back. I heard Sandeep behind us for a while, but we only stopped when we knew we were safe. Clearly there was no love lost between our new friends and us. Looking back, we cracked up over what had happened.

When we reached our hotel that night, there was a guy from Paradise Restaurant,with a note that read, 'There is an outstanding bill of Rs.14,650/- and your friend Sandeep Maheshwari says you will settle it. His group is still with us and will not be released till someone pays the bill.' We had a hearty laugh and I quietly paid him.

Unnati's dying!

Puri was a good couple of days from Hyderabad. However, the prospect of going to the city wasn't rousing and we felt like we were going through the motions more than anything else. But then we cheered each other up that morning as we left Telangana's capital. We reminisced about the incident with the HFJ group.

It was funny as Sandeep seemed like good company. Their entire group did. But then he didn't turn out to be as reliable in money matters. Although I am sure he thought he was being fair in that fight. That's the thing with most people. Every person is a hero in his own mind and in his own life story.

On our way to Puri, we stopped for a night halt at Vishakhapatnam, a coastal city in Andhra Pradesh, heavily influenced by Buddhism. While talking to the manager of our lodge at dinner, he tempted us into hiring a guide the next day and visiting the Borra Caves. We were glad that we took his suggestion, though it meant staying there for two nights instead. The Borra Caves turned out to be an absolute delight. They were natural caves guarded and preserved by the government of Andhra Pradesh, and offered good and natural surroundings in the form of hills and mountains. That's what I loved about our road-trip the most: its best elements were the ones that were unplanned, or those that we encountered mostly by chance. We thanked the manager while checking out and embarked on our journey to Puri.

Frankly, Jagannath Puri, the temple, failed to catch my fancy. I couldn't comprehend how devotees could stand in the humid and hot weather and wait for hours to catch a glimpse of an idol. It may sound like a non-conformist statement, but I'd rather go to the Konark or Puri Beach and play in the sea because despite buying tickets in advance, we had to wait in a queue. Maybe it was all a divine plan by those who controlled the functioning there as a couple of lungi-clad noblemen called 'pandas' noticed our anxiety and approached us. They also eyed our recording equipment which was prohibited inside.

"We have special permission," I directly told as I caught him staring.

"It's great my son. Donate five hundred rupees in the name of the lord and you will get direct darshan of the deity and a special blessing from him!" one said.

The other quickly added, "Another one thousand rupees and you can shoot inside too, son."

They had no clue that their 'son' – which was me – had no interest in spending money there. Sasha joined his hands, gently refusing them. They approached another family behind us. Unnati said, "You are right Ab. It's really not worth it. Now I totally relate to movies like *PK*!

But quickly added, "Since we have come so far, let's wait for some time and just see what it is about."

The eternal-believer and optimist in her won as usual and we finally got our sixty seconds of tete-a-tete with god after two hours of wait.

I prayed saying,

Oh god, give Sashank some self-belief. Give Unnati some fulfillment. And marriage. Give me some sanctity. And yes, if you are really the giver, then please give brains – to all of them who blindly believe in you.

✣

For anyone who has ever taken a long road trip, they will know that there comes a point when you leave your past behind too far, and the future seems too distant. You start breathing the air that is around you at that moment. You only think about the place you are currently at, and the meal you will eat next. That is when you truly start living in your present. I wish we could use this analogy in our everyday lives. After fifty-six days and an eight thousand kilometer long drive, we felt exactly that. I helmed the drive to our next destination. My feelings truly mirrored that of a nomad.

A nomad has more to think of what he will be doing the next moment than to worry about his whole life ahead of him.

I mean, who could have thought we could make such a landmark journey unto this point? We don't know whether we'd ever be able to complete it. But does it matter? No it doesn't.

All we inhaled was the humid sea-breeze that blew around us. Somewhere in our minds, we did think of the day when our journey would end, when Unnati and Sasha would get married, when Bingo Productions would release our movie and when we would all find inner peace. But these thoughts didn't occur to us as frequently as they do in our otherwise regular life.

I had received an email from my boss a couple of days ago, saying that my future in advertising had been permanently jeopardized due to some exit-policies that I had left unfulfilled. Unnati's plight was similar, since she had decided not to continue after returning to Delhi. Sasha, meanwhile, had no interest in his family business. In a way, all three of us would have a fresh start when we would return home.

But it didn't matter to us. We were living in the moment. Maybe it's not enough to say it in words and one has to experience this feeling to know it, but I really left alive.

"Calcutta is a good five hundred kilometers from here!" Unnati said excitedly. It was hard to imagine such pleasure in any of our voices for such a drive when we had started out.

For us, Kolkata, the jewel of the East, was a brief one-night affair. It was more of a gateway to Gosaba in the Sunderbans for us. But who could resist staying longer in our country's former capital city. We ended up staying there for two nights. Unnati's cousin stayed in Kolkata, and for the first time in our trip, we made an exception and stayed with him instead of staying at a hotel – mostly because of her mother's strict insistence since she wanted her nephew to keep an eye on us after the incident in Goa.

"Hey Unns!" he said, hugging her tightly. Vinay, Unnati's cousin, looked like a cool cat.

"Vinay, meet my friends. This is Abhay and that is Sasha…I mean Sashank."

She blushed while introducing him, making it obvious to anyone that something was cooking between them. Vinay turned out to be quite the cool dude and greeted us sportingly. He appreciated our madcap adventure and took us out to dinner at Flurry's, a rather pompous colonial bakery that is now almost synonymous with Kolkata. It was a fantasy that I had shared with Sasha to eat there at least once. After a day in Kolkata's barren heat while visiting the city's landmarks and eating their local food, we couldn't thank Vinay enough for taking us around. Kolkata was a large city and without an insider, we really couldn't have gone to places that he took us to. Finally, it was time to move on to the Sunderbans, a lesser-explored travel destination.

The next day, we set off for our four-hour drive to Gosaba. A large part of the Sunderbans Delta and its mangrove forests are part of Bangladesh. Crazy as we were, Sasha and I had secretly planned to somehow hop-over and claim foot in foreign territory. We told Unnati about our plan just when we were about to reach the park.

"Do you guys have an aggression problem?" she asked.

"What's that like?"

"No, I mean is it some kind of a hormonal rush that you get out of all this? You know, to go look for trouble everywhere we go?"

"Would it make a good movie if it was all hunky-dory? If there is no adventure, there is nothing in it for the viewer," I reasoned. Besides, that was what Bingo's brief was.

"Anyway, how do you intend to do it? I am not saying that I am with you. I just want to know what's on your mind here. The world goes to the Sundarbans to catch a glimpse of the Royal Bengal Tiger, not that I am interested in it after Corbett, but just adding to your informed repertoire," she smirked.

I winked at Sasha. He said, "I have read about a Man Friday there for this kind of an adventure. We just have to find him."

She didn't understand and kept cursing us till we finally reached.

"Once I went in the dense mangrove forest to get honey. That's where I saw a tiger sunbathing near the river. I was so close to him, so I just prayed to our jungle goddess Bonobibi. But the animal smelled me and came near me. It was around three feet from me and started making stalking sounds, as if ready to make an ambush. Running away was not an option. I made scary faces and howled. It was about who succumbed first. When the tiger couldn't get the better of me, it withdrew and silently went into the bushes. By then, I had peed in my pants twice. My throat was bleeding but I had escaped unhurt!" Rafiq recited his amazing story sitting outside the porch of his small house.

Some said he was a Bangladeshi who had migrated because of the lack of employment. Others said he was God's incarnation as he had escaped man-eating tigers many times. Quite a few said he was half-mad. We didn't need to know anything as his track record online showed that he was pretty good. We knew he could help us get on with our crazy adventure.

"Guys, I am telling you it's a stupid idea!" Unnati warned us as we hired Rafiq to be our guide for the next two days in the Sunderbans.

He promised to arrange for video-recording permissions for us and thereby entry in some of its prohibited areas.

Rafiq said, "Why are you worried, madam? I know this jungle like the back of my palm. You want to see the tiger, na? I am the best tracker around, you can ask anyone here!"

Despite our warning, Unnati blurted, "These foolish guys want you to take them across to the Bangladeshi side and come back!"

We stuttered and said, "No, no don't worry, Rafiq Bhai."

He laughed and said, "Sir, there are poor villagers who go across almost every other day just to find wood, honey, better fish and a better livelihood. And here, you want to go for the sake of fun! I don't mind at all. What's a border anyway? It is an imaginary line between two countries!"

The next day, we started out early, even before the sun had risen. It was completely dark outside, except for the sounds of fireflies and crickets. Rafiq wanted to reach the point where the Indian part of Sundarbans ended before daybreak. He prayed to their goddess and urged us to do so too. The locals believed that it would help them encounter the tiger.

We got onto a steamboat. We crossed a little river before coming to the point where we'd be entering the dense mangrove forest. After the night at Alwar, somehow, nothing scared me anymore. Rafiq was happy to find some brave accomplices.

"Look at those trees on our left, sir. They are shorter than usual. This marks the start of the core area of the Sundarbans where most of our tigers live."

Unnati shuddered at the mention of the animal. She asked, "How many tigers are there? What are the chances of one being around?" Fear gripped her voice when she asked this. Sasha and I continued to walk quietly behind our guide.

Rafiq laughed and said, "Around 4000 square kilometers belongs to India, and the last estimate suggested there were a hundred tigers. That means one for every forty square kilometers. That's like one per village. Anyway, we don't trust these government figures. We go by our instinct. Given Abhay sir's and Sashank sir's enthusiasm, my instinct told me this morning that we will get to see one!"

"What!" Unnati almost shrieked.

"Relax madam, that's why Rafiq is with you."

She kept mum after that. We were not even going to shoot on Bangladesh territory, and therefore were making a joy-trip to say the least. She had every option to not come this morning.

Honestly, the jungle looked mesmerizing from that close. Even if we were not to go across the border, this trip was worth every rupee. No safari in Corbett or any other damn place could come close to walking in the forests with nothing but an experienced old pro without any weapons in hand. At 5 a.m., the sky was dark blue above with very little light penetrating from those dense bushes. The trees were constantly swaying due to a strong breeze. On one side, there was a river flowing, making its presence felt by the sound of running water. On the other side, there were howls and other sounds of animals every now and then. Though we were walking in a huddle, I felt alone and aware of the fact that we had left our resort and the park's safety zone far behind.

"This is the river we have to cross by boat. We call it the 'Badi nadi', which means big river. This separates the two countries. But remember, this is like the border here, so we have to be very careful. There may be surveillance navy boats that might catch us. If they do, just say that we lost our way while making an early morning documentary on fishing practices here." Rafiq told us as we finally reached the banks and were ready to board his little speedboat.

Then, he introduced his accomplice, "This is Pitru, he knows his way around there and will go with you in his little jeep."

He was a little Bangla guy who probably crossed the border very early in the morning and now was there, ready to navigate us.

"Guys, think one last time. We don't have to do this. There is nothing to prove to anyone. You can't even tell anyone about this as it's illegal!" Unnati warned us one last time.

The birds were chirping loudly and it appeared that daylight would break anytime. Sasha comforted her, "Hey, don't worry, Unns. We will just go there, get off at the bank and stay for half-an-hour or so and then come back."

The boat navigated on a fast tide as we sat in it without speaking a word to each other. Rafiq handled the routing and sat at the end with the engine. The river felt more significant than it was. It divided a forest into two different countries although people on either side spoke the same language, worked in similar professions, and were equally afraid of tigers.

Suddenly, there was a hooter buzz. Rafiq panicked hearing it and shouted, "It must be the navy boat. I don't know which side it is from. Duck under and I will move faster!"

Without any time to think, we ducked. He increased the speed. From the corner of my eyes, I could see a large boat at a distance that probably blew the hooter. Rafiq was quick and made our boat move awkwardly towards the other end. He disembarked and starting pulling it. Then, he dropped a pair of heavily roped tyres in the water and yelled to us saying, "Run, run fast and get inside! If those cops are from the Indian side, they will not come here. If they are Bangladeshi, they'll probably come, search and go back after a while. Either way, come back exactly after an hour. Otherwise, I will leave without you!" We looked at each other and couldn't make sense of what he said.

"Leave without us? So will he really leave us here? Without our passports?" Unnati asked in terror.

"No, Unns! Again, we are not migrating. Let's just run now!" Sasha and Unnati followed suit. We followed Pitru, who had run into the bushes and was behind his engine, preparing the little adventure for all of us. We stepped on the bank and though there was no proof that we were on foreign land, what mattered was that we knew that we were. Sasha and I opened our arms wide and smiled. We glanced at each other, sharing the high we had experienced when we had cleared our Class XII board exams.

Unnati broke my trance and pushed me. I saw Rafiq getting out of sight and the hooter seemed to be getting louder. It meant that whoever blew it had followed us. I started running. Sasha and Unnati did too. We entered the dense jungle and got into the jeep, even though there was nothing foreign or distinctly Bangladeshi about it. Sitting in the car, we let Pitru navigate the bushes. Unnati was sweating the most. Suddenly, a huge spotlight fell on us from somewhere far. It didn't give us time to think or react, but at least it wasn't from the river's side.

I shouted at Pitru, "Drive fast!"

The poor guy was startled. He started driving like a maniac. Suddenly, he slammed the brakes and the jeep came to a screeching halt. All three of us sat with our mouths wide open, as it took us a while to gather why he had stopped. There was an orange object crossing the path in front of our jeep. It walked slowly, stepping out of the bushes on our left and lingered to the middle of the road. It was huge and confirmed our fears.

"Sher Khan!" said Unnati in terror.

Sher Khan heard her and stopped, staring at the headlights of our jeep. It looked bigger than I could have ever imagined it would be. I pushed Pitru lightly, as a gesture to dim the headlights but he was too flabbergasted to do anything. The tiger decided to sit on the road and yawn, enjoying the extra light in an otherwise dim early morning. We didn't dare to breathe loudly. It was hardly ten feet away from our vehicle and we could hear its nostrils flaring and making grunting sounds, like it had found his breakfast and could attack us any moment.

Finally, poor Pitru regained his instincts and started reversing the jeep slowly. As the animal saw the movement, it became alert and got up. Suddenly, the hooter's sound fell on our ears. We were stuck between the border police on one side and a tiger on the other. I didn't have my camera. Otherwise, what happened in the next few seconds could have been my entry to Oscars. Pitru was threatened by the hooter's sound and pressed the accelerator of his jeep, surging forward at full throttle. Neither the tiger nor any of us expected him to react so foolishly. In the next couple of seconds, the jeep hit the wild cat that roared louder than one can imagine. Sasha shouted at Pitru but the damage was done. Our jeep couldn't slow down in time and hit a tree. Unnati toppled in the air and fell right next to the tiger on the ground.

She yelled in pain, "Aaaaaah.".

For a split second, I thought the tiger would take its revenge and tear her into pieces. Luckily, the continuous sound of the hooter seemed to have scared him. It got up and slowly labored his way into the bush. Perhaps its body and ego had both got bruised badly that day.

Unnati lay on the ground, crying, as her leg had hit a big rock. Within minutes, a few army men surrounded us. I had no clue which side they were from, but they were more sympathetic seeing a girl weeping in pain, rather than being angry at our intrusion.

"We... We are sorry..." Sasha started pleading immediately on seeing them.

"Relax, let us get her help first!" One of them replied and their team pulled Unnati up. They escorted her back to the shore on a stretcher. I saw Rafiq sitting on the boat. He helped us climb into the boat again and thanked the army men for their kindness.

As he navigated the boat back, he told us, "Those were Bangladeshi cops. They found me, but I cooked up a story of losing the way and also told them of a tourist group who had accompanied me. That's why they went looking for you. It is very usual here so they just warned that it should never happen again. How did madam get injured?"

Sasha and I sat opposite each other. Unnati's cousin, Vinay, stood next to us in a hospital room in Kolkata. Her mother was on the phone, and it was on speaker mode.

"How dare you take my daughter to an expedition like that! Sashank, you! Look at you! I sent her on this road trip because of you. This is what you do, you drug addict! And your friend, that rich, spoilt brat! It is my mistake after all! I should never have believed smooth talkers like him. Go to hell, both of you! I just want to see my daughter back. ASAP. She should not die because of you morons. Vinay, are you listening?"

"Yes, Mausi, I am here. Listen, I think it was an accident…" he tried to pacify her.

"Don't tell me what you think. Just get my daughter back to me. Catch the first flight and do whatever you must. Or I will come there…" and she started weeping loudly.

"Don't worry, Mausi! It's not that bad an injury. I know my way here. I will fly her to Delhi tonight. You take care!" He hung up. Thank god he did. Yeah, she was her mother, but she was being too hysterical, I'd say.

Sasha didn't think so, though. His face stiffened, and he pulled me outside.

"Unnati is dying!" he shouted.

"Are you nuts? It's just a minor fracture."

"What do you mean it's a minor fracture? She has been silent for the past couple of hours now."

"That's because the doctor injected her. Listen bhai, you calm down. Let's arrange for her to go back first. We will discuss it later," I told him.

"Why is she here? Because I wanted to be Sunny Deol and cross the border," he kept cursing himself as we walked back to her room. The only sane person around, Vinay, had thankfully made enough calls to take it on from there.

Lama for life

We sat and ate in silence at a place that was midway between Kolkata and Gaya, close to Dhanbad. It was a fairly large city and we were surrounded by the hustle-bustle of buses, rickshaw-pullers, carts and people near the restaurant where we had stopped. We felt burdened with guilt. We had barely spoken since we started our drive that morning. Finally, he broke the ice, "This time we really messed up, didn't we?"

I wondered how many times we had said that to each other during the trip. I thought we had messed up by hiring a drunkard at Corbett, or when we had driven to Ladakh without acclimatizing to the high altitude. Or, was it the havoc at Wagah that was the biggest mess up? Wait, what about our staying at Bhangarh Fort all night? Losing our car to marshy sand? Goa? Hyderabad's Paradise Restaurant? But was it all worth it? What did we do in the Sundarbans? We almost lost Unnati! We should have called the trip off already!

"Any word from Delhi?" I asked him.

"Obviously her mother won't let her speak to me or you after what happened. I called her sister and she said Unns was doing okay. She is on bed rest for a minimum of twenty-four hours. We will only be able to speak to her tomorrow," he said.

How will they ever get married now was the first thought I had as he spoke. Which mother will let her daughter marry a guy who risked her daughter's as well as his own life for that kind of a kick? They'd have to wait and see.

"Ab, I want to go home," Sasha said.

"I know. Me too. But hey, I won't stop you. Seriously, if you want to, chuck everything and go to Patna. Take a flight from there and be by her side."

He looked up from his plate with wet eyes. I offered him a hug and he took it. We left our unconsumed litthi-chokhas and went back to the car. At least she was fine. Her injury wasn't that serious. It was just the shock of what had happened and the thought of how much worse it could have been. I wondered if Unnati's mother was right when she said on the phone that I was a rich, spoilt brat.

"Did you inform Tanya?" Sasha asked, as he took over the wheel.

"No, I don't think it's appropriate to do so yet," I told him. We drove in silence again.

❖

We reached Gaya late in the evening, without stopping for a breather or dinner. We went straight to our guide's house and then to Bodh Gaya, the most important pilgrimage site for Buddhists across the world. It is said that Gautam Buddha found enlightenment sitting under a tree there. We hoped that having spent the day without any food would lessen the impact of our unpleasant experiences and enlightenment would be closer. It was strange to be without Unnati that day. When you spend so much time in each other's company, and that too share many defining moments, it is extremely difficult to adjust when that person suddenly leaves.

It was a dream we cherished. The three of us dreamed of completing this journey together. We had made such elaborate plans for the last few days and Unnati had a vital part to play in them. Our movie was also going to seem incomplete and disconnected without her. The worst part was that she was in pain because we had wanted an adventure. Damn!

Our guide had arranged an early morning session with Yonten Kondala, a lama visiting the Mahabodhi Temple around that time. He was a famous pupil of the Dalai Lama. It was an opportunity to document something different. Now, however, we desperately needed his wisdom.

I woke up at 4:30 a.m. the next morning, and as was asked, took a cold shower before proceeding to meet him. I held my camera while Sasha took the mic, filling in for Unnati.

He sat outside under a large tree on a platform, and looked like a sixty-year-young man. I presumed he was about sixty because he wore thick glasses and had very little hair on his head along with lines criss-crossing his face. I say 'young' because his face shone and exuded light. I went ahead and touched his feet before settling down on a mat.

He said very gently, "You don't need to do that. I am no saint; I am just a teacher. My name is Yonten Kondala. Please introduce yourself, son."

Sasha and I introduced ourselves. A couple of other guests said their names and sat down on the mat.

"My apologies for making you wake this early. I have to catch a train at ten. I promise I will be as honest as I can, and try to introduce and impart all practical truths that my mentor, the great Dalai Lama, has taught me. Trust these principles as universal. You can apply them in your daily lives. I have been told that one of you wants to make a recording of this session to be later used in a movie. I will be glad to let that happen. Just one request, keep it original."

His voice was so soft yet commanding, that it seemed like an order from the Almighty.

"Yes, sir," I replied and focused my camera. Sasha positioned the mic on a stand in front of him.

He said again, "Sashank, you look tense. You must first relax and surrender yourself completely to this conversation. All of you must do so. Only then, what I say will make sense to you, and your heart will absorb it."

Not knowing how to react, Sasha folded his hands and went back to his place. I put my camera on auto-record mode.

The lama said, "Even your friend here, Abhay, his face has trouble written all over it. Why do you guys look so glum? If I am not too intrusive, may I ask for the reason?"

Sasha said, "Sir, because of our stupidity, our friend had a terrible accident a couple of days ago. She was otherwise supposed to be here today, but had to fly back to our hometown. And our mistake is unpardonable."

He smiled. "Son, firstly don't call me sir. If you find it disrespectful to address me by my name, you can call me Lama. Next, how would you know if your mistake is pardonable or not? How do you even know if it was a mistake or not? Maybe it was her destiny to have been caught in that accident. Don't presume things. Let time decide these matters."

"But sir," I cut him, "I mean, Lama, we were the ones who caused the circumstances that led to the accident. Even if it was her destiny, we are to blame for getting her there."

He smiled again. His smile was magnetic and soothing. "Dear Abhay, have you ever seen a bird fly? I am sure you have. When a bird flies high, too high, and suddenly bumps into an electric pole and dies from high voltage, is it a mistake of the engineer who erected that pole? Or the minister who approved the pole's location? Or the guy sitting at the electricity board office who saw it on his CCTV but didn't do anything? Or the millions of people who use power from the pole? Who would you blame for that bird's death?"

"I don't understand you, Lama."

"My son, it is the bird's fate to die like this. No one could have changed it. No one is to take the blame, either. We are all a part of this karma system. Whatever we do now, it will essentially set the universe in motion to effect its consequence. It may happen today, tomorrow or after decades. So don't fall into this guilt trap; your friend was destined to be there."

I questioned back, "But why were we, her friends, the catalysts for causing trouble to our own loved one?"

He reasoned, "I don't know. Maybe it's your old karma that led you to see pain of your near one."

There was silence at his reply.

The Bengali lady raised her hand for a question, "Lama, if like this, the bad elements of our country can go about doing killings and causing terrorism and what not, and later on say your own karma led to your suffering?"

She made a good point.

He said, "My daughter, first you need to decode god to understand this. There are many belief systems about him in our world. Buddhism believes that bad things happen because we tend to get attached to worldly pleasures in our quest for contentment. Therefore suffering happens because of our own sin of getting attached."

He added, "Instead of questioning why something bad has happened, we must accept it as a temporary thing or a feeling and move on. Let the sinner's fate be decided by its own due course. You just listen to your inner voice. The first voice that comes out of your heart – it is usually of truth, of god. I am a follower of nontheism but would still advocate following your heart or your god, whichever way you like to see it."

This man was binding us with his magical tongue.

I elbowed Sasha to ask from the list of questions that we had. Lama caught me doing so and gently said, "Son, I think of myself as much as a teacher to you as to him. So you ask whatever you have to without hesitation."

I questioned him, "Lama, you explained beautifully about how karma works. Then what is god, why did he even send us here? What is the purpose of our life, of our existence?"

He quickly said, "Please don't be so resetless. Have some tea." He sipped his own while we also sipped the mystical tea from bowls placed in front of us.

"When you had to lift that tea cup, what did you do? Your brain asked your hand to lift it while it also asked your mouth to open itself. Your nose was filled with its therapeutic aroma while your mouth became full of bittersweet ginger flavor. These actions, these senses are there and we trust they will remain as they are. This trust, this faith is god."

It took a while to understand what he meant, but then the foreigner, one of the visitors, summed it, "So I am god, and god is me. It is our faith, and not in a scripture or idol."

Lama smiled in approval. It made sense. He added, "Just as everybody's encounter with school, or parents or friend is different, so is each person's experience and relationship with god."

I asked further, "Lama, how do I know what my purpose is?"

He said, "Abhay, you don't have to look too far outside. For now, your purpose is to find happiness. If you look for happiness, your inner voice itself will navigate you on the route of your existential purpose. Just go with the flow. Identify what makes you happy and follow it whole-heartedly. Don't look around too much. There may be someone whose purpose is different from yours, and therefore some other things make him happy. It shouldn't mean anything to you."

This time Sasha got serious and asked him, "But Lama, everyone in this world is after money. Whatever one does, the end result is measured by how much money he made. Whoever has more money can certainly buy more comforts for himself – eventually leading to a happier life too." The pain in his voice of constantly being looked down by his family was evitable.

"Don't judge, my son. I told you earlier, let your karma be the consequence and not a judgement. Now, if you think anyone is happier than you because he or she has more money, please tell me about that person." he replied.

"Abhay," he said. I turned around to look at him.

But Sasha continued looking at Lama and said, "Abhay is my childhood friend and has always had more riches. He is never bound by any responsibilities or anything else. He can wake up at 11:00 a.m. or sleep past midnight. He doesn't have to worry about any material things ever. Even this trip is largely sponsored by him because he has more money."

I had no clue where it all came from. Almost eleven years of friendship and I had never known what he thought of me. I continued to stare back at Lama blankly. Lama's eyes met mine and looked assuring. He said, "What if I were to tell you that Abhay doesn't care about it and is actually looking for ways to expand his life beyond this?" he kept looking at me.

I blurted, "Yeah, it's true. If anything, I always thought Sasha was happier, because he had a large family and has found his true love." Now it was Sasha's turn to be confused.

Lama said, "Boys, I know how it is, especially at your age. You are too close to each other, and that's why sometimes, such comparisons creep in. However, don't let this ruin anything. As I said, life's path and purpose is different for both of you. And so should your definition of happiness be. Sashank, ask yourself, would earning loads of money really make you happy? If it will, then go for it with all of your heart and don't regret your decision. There are some happy souls who have a lot of wealth, though they have to slog fifty-sixty hours a week, and it's really okay.

"At the same time, if you really think getting buckets of money or fame only make you happy, then it is a hollow approach. Okay ask yourself: somebody writes you a cheque of a hundred million dollars. Wow! What next? You will go about spending a lot of it, right? But you will eventually tire down and start thinking of ways to grow it more, otherwise you will run out of it. Then you will start looking at things that interest you, maybe starting a school or running a business or writing a book – that's the moment you are at right now." He paused.

Looking at our confused faces, he said, "Yes, you are right now at that stage. You all have limited time left in life form. That's your real wealth, your real money. After spending half of your wealth in my previous example, you start thinking of how to utilize the rest.

"Why not substitute your time with that hundred million instead. You guys must be what twenty-five or thirty? We all have an average active life of about eighty years. By that logic, you only have about fifty years left. Make the most of it. If you had to start a business to expand your leftover wealth, why not do it now?"

Lama further added, "Define success on your own terms. Our creator didn't inscribe 'success = money/fame' on a famous wall or a tomb anywhere on this planet. It is we, humans who predefine it as that. But you make your own definition of success and go full throttle to get it.

"Did I tell you what success was to me when I was your age? I had to meet my hero, to serve him and to learn from him. The great Dalai Lama. Around thirty years back when I managed to meet him, I went back home and wrote a full page in my day's diary – 'Today was the most successful day of my life. I wish I can build on it and make every single day successful from here on.' I still keep that diary with me."

There was complete silence as he stopped speaking. By the looks on everyone's faces, it was clear that all four people sitting there had learnt invaluable lessons in that session.

Finally I broke the silence and asked him, "You are right, Lama. Please guide me about how I will find my purpose, rather my happiness? I have been a wayward person and have had no real direction to my life so far."

He smiled again and said, "My son, I am afraid no preacher or lama can ever do that for you. This difficult task has to be performed by your own self. But I can show you the path of getting there."

I nodded. I was willing to follow him.

So he continued, "First, you have to slow down and stop living in the fast lane. Do lesser things, make lesser commitments. You must. You shouldn't expect to win the world. If you are busy doing that, you can never have time to be with your inner self and to find that happiness meant for you.

"Secondly, you should let go of all your possessions. Material and otherwise, including your own body. Be detached, yet enjoy things that are yours at the same time. It's a difficult balance, but somehow you have to own and disown everything at the same time. They are all temporary. I think meditation should help.

"Third, be full of gratitude and thankfulness to every single person and / or source of energy that you are aware of. Express this gratitude at every given opportunity. I don't mean to only people known to you, although they count the most.

"Thank the sun for giving this light to you every single day. Thank the water you drink which eradicates your thirst. Thank the random child whose smile makes you laugh yourself."

He looked around at the others and continued, "The above is true for all of you. But for this last point, Abhay and Sashank, you are the luckier ones. For you have each other. From what I understand, you've known each other for long and are thick friends. You really have a closer confidante to help you find your happiness other than your own self – that is each other. You can be of help to each other in finding that path of happiness, as a mentor and as a companion. We all need that 'someone' in our lives to join us on this path of happiness, be it a friend, sibling, spouse or parent. It's a blessing to have found such friendship. Think about it and I am sure you will be able to find me before I leave the temple."

He folded his hands and went into a meditative pose for the next couple of minutes. Everyone followed him and spent some time reflecting on this session. When we opened our eyes, he was not on the elevated platform anymore.

❖

Sasha and I kept sitting there while the other two left. I kept staring at him, still thinking about what to say and where to start. I broke down and said, "I am sorry brother."

"What? No, why are you sorry? I am sorry I always thought you were luckier because you had rich parents. I have been so stupid."

"No, that's nothing. As I confessed to Lama, I had always been jealous of you, and of those beautiful relationships in your life. I never had any family."

"Bhai, you are my family too!" he said and hugged me. We cried like school kids, and it was probably due since the accident at Sundarbans. We had trifled our tears for Unnati's sake. Now it was difficult to hold them back any further.

After a while, we mellowed down and came back to our senses. I spoke first, "Sasha, before I lose this feeling that the lama just put me in, I want to make another confession. A more serious and specific one this time. But as he said, you deserve to know this. I tried telling you this earlier also, but I think I didn't communicate it well enough then... It was I who messed up in Goa, deliberately. I bribed the manager to cause all that havoc in your love life. I have been terrible to you. I did it all because I thought I had something for Unnati. I feel like a fool now admitting this. I am a bad, bad person and really do not deserve a friend like you!" I started crying again.

After listening to me patiently and letting me sob a little, he slapped me. I was in a bit of a shock as I felt my right jaw shake. But I deserved it. Then he said, "I knew it already. I found out when we were on the road to Hyderabad. Don't ask me how and why, but Unnati and I had this conversation about Goa.

"I rewound everything in my mind and called the hotel manager when you were busy eating dinner. I threatened him and got him to tell me. It was easy to connect the dots thereafter. I didn't confront you then otherwise Unnati would have created a scene. This slap was overdue since then."

My tears stopped. I kept looking at him for some anger, but there was none.

"Hey, forget it, it happens. Besides, you motivated me to reunite with her and this time, made it even better. I'd have never had the balls to propose to her for marriage otherwise!" He brushed it off like it was nothing. "Actually if it's about confessions, I have another one to make. But promise me, you will do what I ask you to."

"Oh just say it!" I was ready to do anything.

"I read your Nani's letter secretly, in Goa. Please call your mother, for her sake, for your Nani's sake, and for my sake," he said folding his hands like he was begging for candy.

I paused and stammered, "I knew that already too. I overheard you talking to Unns about it."

"Fucker! Is there anything in this world you do not know?" He grinned and continued, "Bhai, don't think. Just do it. As lama said, we need to trust each other and help find our purposes and roads to happiness. I won't be lying if I say that the way to your destination starts with making this call. I know there is much agony inside you. Maybe it will help heal it all. Do it!"

He kept pushing me. I took out my mobile phone and dialed her number. Strangely enough, I still remembered it.

She picked it after the second ring, "Abhay! I can't really believe it's you. How are you, my son? Is everything fine with your trip?"

Her voice had the concern that I had always been longing for. I choked a little. However, within seconds, all my frustration at being discarded by her came back. I spoke in my usual stone-hearted tone. "Yes, I am doing okay. Listen, I got Nani's parcel and it had a letter in it." I wanted to know if she knew anything about it first.

"Oh that's great! Your Nani loved you very much. What did the letter say?" She probably didn't know anything about that letter at all. Or perhaps it was Lama's effect that I had become too trusting all of a sudden.

"It was just a letter in general. Listen, Mom. I don't know how to say this. But okay, I... I just wanted to see you once. I shall be back in Delhi next week. If you are around, I will come over." The words came out of my mouth with great difficulty.

There was no response from her. Then, I heard her cry. In between sobs, she said, "I want to meet you too, Abhay. Anytime is good time to meet my son. You just let me know when you want to come. I am in Varanasi now for an exhibition. I will come back whenever you reach Delhi and want to meet. Just let me know I am so happy and eager."

I couldn't hide my emotions for too long, either. "Okay! I will call you when I am in Delhi. Okay, bye!" I said and put the phone down without her response.

"I heard everything. You fool, she is in Varanasi now. We will leave for Varanasi tomorrow. Meet her there. Don't wait for next week. That's what your Nani also wanted," Sasha said.

"You really think my Nani was right? That Mom has had a tough time?" I asked, still full of emotion.

"How would I know? Hey, the lama said to leave it to your karma. Just listen to your inner voice and follow it whole-heartedly."

"Thanks, man. Thanks so much for making me do this. I now know why I never had a sibling, because God made you fill that spot in my life." I hugged him again. From crying, to confessing, to finding fulfillment, the last half an hour had seen it all. "Sasha. Can I say something?"

"Oh, just say it!"

"Now, it is your turn. Promise me, that when we get back to Delhi, you will not wait for a 'D-day' and will ask Unnati to marry you the next month. No need for an auspicious date or kundli or the wedding season or shraad or whatever. Nothing! I will decide a date next month and you will both get married that day!"

He looked through me, scratched his head and then smiled. "Given the situation that she is in, her parents... Do you think it's going to be that easy?"

"It will never be easy. But together, we will make it happen. Promise me you will do it."

His eyes said he would do anything. He too had a hangover from that session. I said, "Also, promise me that you will open that halwai shop."

"You can't be serious, Ab!"

"The lama said leave it to your karma. Just hear your inner voice and follow it whole-heartedly!"

If years can make someone mature, I wondered how many mornings like this would make me win a Noble prize. Within a few hours, I was guilt-free regarding my best friend. I had spoken to my mother and was finally going to meet her. Overall, I had a fresh perspective for the rest of my life to come. Sasha regretted that Unnati couldn't attend this life-altering session. I assured him that getting married in itself would work like therapy for her. As for him, well, married men don't stand much of a chance.

On a serious note, we both felt the need to thank Yonten Kondala, our lama for life. We went around the temple to seek him out. However, we were disappointed when an elderly gentleman at a desk told us that he had left for the station to catch a train to Patna. But before leaving, he had left a message for us, to be given to us if we came looking for him. "I guess it must be you guys!" said the gentleman.

"Yes!" we shouted in excitement.

"Well, he told me to tell you to go and take a stroll in the Mahabodhi Temple starting from the Bodhi tree and then going to each and every nuke nook and corner of the temple. Then, in our meditation park, take a hut and meditate for an hour. Before you start meditating, think about the purpose that you've discovered and the lecture that the lama gave this morning."

"That's all? Can we have his phone number or something, because there is something important we need to tell him too!" I said.

He grinned and said, "Lama doesn't carry a phone like we do. If he had deemed it important to speak, he would have left a way for you to contact him. Why do you think he left only this message?"

It made sense. Disappointed, we left and went to take a round that he wished. The temple was very beautiful, and had several legendary spots where Gautam Buddha is believed to have meditated and spent his time. He attained enlightenment while sitting for forty-nine days straight under the Bodhi tree. It was difficult to imagine someone sitting this way for such a long time, when a couple of hours with a lama can enlighten you as well. I guess that's where the beauty of Buddhism was.

For the first time in my life, I had actually felt so involved and liberated inside a temple premise. I felt myself being slowly transformed and losing my skepticism as I gathered more knowledge about Buddha and his thoughts. It wasn't confirmed if Buddhism was to become my calling, but at least there was some belief generating somewhere. Finally, we meditated or rather, tried to meditate, and then thought about our decisions that we took for our future earlier in the day. I imagined meeting my mother. How did she look now? Why did Nani want me to meet her? What would I say to her? Hating her was easier than facing her or hearing her out with an open mind.

Meeting @ full circle

"How come we've reached Maharashtra?" I asked.

"What?" He woke from his slumber. I can't believe I had let this bozo drive early in the morning. Despite his recent benevolence, I couldn't trust his IQ – not in this book at least.

We stopped by the roadside and stared at the signboard again. It read 'Aurangabad – 05 KM.' We had started out from Gaya in the morning and the next state after Bihar should have been Uttar Pradesh, fair and square. We navigated quite early on NH-2 and were confused how this had happened.

"You must have been thinking about Unnati. I didn't tell you to fantasize! I just said I would give you both a date," I scolded him.

"Usually, I don't trust my map skills either, but this is bizarre. I swear I didn't take any unusual turn. We have barely been driving for an hour-and-a-half!" he reasoned.

It took us a while to realize that we were still on NH-2 and what we were staring at was a small town with the same name as the one in Maharashtra. This one was in Bihar though, and its only fame to glory was that it belonged to the Magadha Empire in history.

However, after having 'discovered' it, it was impossible for us to not pay a visit, albeit a short one. It turned out to be like any other town in Bihar – backward, hot and divided on race. We discovered this last sad part as we sat for an early brunch at Hotel

Shambhavi, the only decent-looking highway establishment. But its food was average, there was better litti-chokha and sattu found on every other street throughout the state. When we asked our waiter to get us some taash kebabs instead, he returned with a sorry face and said that the chef was offended and was not going to take a request from me, as I was a Rajbanshi. He asked if we could make our appeal directly to him.

"What class is your chef then?" Sasha quizzed.

"He is a Yadav, from the Ahir caste," the waiter said, bowed and returned.

We ate our food in silence. Both of us had no idea of what our class or caste was in terms of the hierarchy. It was a touchy subject, so it didn't seem appropriate to ask or verify. After eating for a while, Sasha whispered to me, "What class would Lama Yontan be? I am sure he won't be served any food here till he produces his certificate."

"Shut up and get going quickly. We aren't in Bodhgaya anymore!" I told him.

The ride to Varanasi was smooth. But, without Unnati, the journey wasn't even half as enjoyable as it used to be. 'Two's company, three is a crowd' is a statement for loners. We really missed our third musketeer. Our only consolation was that we were less than a week from getting back home and finishing this epic journey.

I looked outside, rolling the windowpanes down to let the summer heat and the breeze carrying the occasional smell of cowdung to float in.

Like earlier, my mind started digressing from the past and the future, and had come back to the present. Even Lama, who we had met just the previous day, seemed like a distant memory. There is something mysteriously beautiful about our country. Just like its people, its climate and culture change from state to state. So could be our state of mind if one takes a road-trip. Really the landscape changes every fifty kilometers!

Varanasi or Benaras or Kashi, the most important city for believers of Hinduism, came into view. From our car, which was at a distance, it looked like a painting. There were large temples parallel to River Ganga. There were people of all kinds taking baths, shooting photos, eating, strolling or just moving about slowly. All of this was against the backdrop of noisy shops. It seemed a little like Haridwar. If comparisons could be made, Varanasi seemed busier and more like a spiritual supermarket.

"Unnati would have loved to be here. Look at these snake charmers! Amazing," Sasha said, as we posed near a guy playing with huge snakes and pythons around his neck. We clicked our selfie for the Varanasi chapter with him. Somebody had to take Unnati's place, after all. We tired ourselves out for the rest of the day by strolling around in the local markets. In the evening, watching the Varanasi aarti was as claustrophobic an experience as it had been at Haridwar because of the crowds. I don't know what thrill people get in being pushed around in a crowd, in sweating, being crushed, and having very little air to breathe, just to catch a glimpse of some fat priests performing a ritual of worship. If you love God so much as to praise him, can't you do it in a little more comfort?

It was obvious that at some point, Sasha and I would break away from each other in this crowd. With very little interest in recording the procession, I drifted to a chaat shop.

Then, I remembered that my mother was in town, too. I decided to go visit her unannounced, and surprise her. My inner voice said I should do it without thinking twice. How would I find out where she was? Should I call or text her and ask? If I did either, it wouldn't be a surprise.

I remembered how I had taken a dip in the sacred river at Haridwar, but ended up being disturbed thinking about my parents' divorce instead. It is said that life comes a full circle in its own strange way. I hoped that taking another dip in the river would complete that circle for me. I walked ahead to the emptier side of the ghats and looked for a spot where I could get wet. It was well into the evening. The dark sky ensured very less visibility. As I climbed down a couple of steps, I saw a man wearing saffron, meditating, with his back to me. He had a fire burning in front of him. Curiously, I went near him to see what ritual he was performing. When I came to the side, I saw him talking softly to a woman bowing opposite him. On a closer look, I grew numb from the shock of what I saw. It was my mother!

She had grown older from when I had last seen her. She seemed weaker, too. The old priest was explaining something to her, and she continued nodding.

Realizing that there was someone close by, they stopped. The man looked at me. My mother, too, as if woken from a spell, looked up. It took her a while to realize that it was me.

"Abhay!" she shrieked happily. The priest probably realized who I was, as he too smiled at hearing my name. She got up and hugged me.

I was overwhelmed with emotion on seeing her, and embraced her tightly. I had had no time to plan my meeting with her. Maybe this was my full circle, and I didn't need the dip anymore.

"Oh! I am so happy to finally see you. I... I will die of happiness, son!" she exclaimed. One really can't fake contentment; it was genuine.

"But you were here for business, right? What's all this? What is this priest for?" I asked.

The priest got up. He placed his hand on her head and said, "Sujata, you don't need me now. I will talk to you later!" Turning to me, he said, "God bless you, my son!" and walked away from that place.

I looked at her for answers. She said, "I will tell you everything. Sit! Let my eyes soak in the sight of you. I am seeing you after so many years. You've grown so handsome. This little moustache suits you so well. I always had at least three or four different pictures of you in my mind for so long a time..."

I cut her short. "If you thought so much about me, why did you leave me?" I was back to the basics.

She turned away to gaze at the river. A huge plume of smoke blew in the air from a fire at a distance. "Abhay, I was like this smoke to you and your father. It was important only till it was a part of that fire. Once it separated, it became meaningless."

I remembered my Nani's letter. I sat on a stair below to hold her knees. "Mom, no guessing games anymore. I know you must have had your reasons for the fight with Dad. I want to know it all. I know that there is a lot you've hidden from me, especially your pain. Tell me exactly what had happened."

She looked at me with wet eyes. Usually, I used to become impatient whenever she ended up crying like this on the phone, which was, well, all the time. But now, I was adamant and kept rubbing her knees to comfort her. Finally, she asked, "Who told you about this?"

"A son can read his mother's mind and her pain. This connection was created by our karma," I said emotionally.

She wiped her tears now, and said, rubbing my head. "I know you are intelligent. I knew you'd understand me. Trust me, without questioning. Had I known that you would start hating me, I'd have told you this back then. I am sorry, my son. You are right, I am the reason you've spent all your life mistrusting people and relationships."

Hearing her reading my problems, I got sentimental and broke down too. She said, "Don't cry. I will tell you everything."

She heaved a deep sigh and began, "You know my marriage with your dad wasn't a smooth one. We always kept getting on each other's nerves, to the point that he indulged in infidelity. I had found out long ago that he was having an affair with a colleague. You were very little back then, around seven or eight. I cried, but did not confront him. That was my first mistake. He took it as acceptance. Then, he discarded me completely. To the world, we lived like a family, like a couple, but in reality, we were never together. I lived my life in hope after that. He kept ignoring me to a point that I went through a period where I stopped valuing myself. You were too young to talk to and were busy in your own world. I had nobody except for a friend or two to discuss my situation with. I was needed only to cook for your father or to look after you. Then, I made the second mistake. Burdened by the disregard for so many years and consumed by the needs of a woman's body, I made a silly mistake with a random person at a party. It is all too difficult to tell you today, son, but I hope you will understand. It wasn't that I looked for a relationship outside that broken marriage, but that day, I just gave in to my physical needs. Alas, that affair gave me not only a stained mind and guilt, but as I was to discover six months later, it gave me AIDS."

"What?"

She began crying again. "Yes. Now you can understand, given the stigma around it, can you?"

I was silent.

"How could I tell the world that I was HIV positive? I didn't care about myself. But the social isolation you would have faced would have been terrible had I chosen to live with you. My divorce with your father was anyways inevitable and we had decided we would file for it when you would turn eighteen. Besides leaving you to live with him, I had no other choice," she said.

"Does Dad know?"

"Would he have cared? You think I'd need to tell him?" Her rock eyes shunned me. She had suffered a lot, clearly. "Son, I never told it to anyone. Not my brothers or sister or anyone else. Only my mother, your Nani, knew. She never raised a finger on me and trusted me blindly. I had this feeling that my son would trust me too, and I may never have to explain why I deserted him," she said. I felt useless.

She continued, "Thankfully I got tested at the right time and atleast I can continue to live a healthy life till there is a permanent cure found. It takes traveling to America a few times and intense treatment for long, which has not only wiped off most of my savings, but also my confidence. That's why I started coming to Varanasi for some peace and awakening. That priest you just met was my spiritual guru. Mostly he asks me about my emotional problems and tries to cheer me up. Today, he told me that he will never see me again, and that I should meet you. And suddenly you were standing there! It was nothing but God's miracle."

I couldn't control myself. I immediately hugged her tight and cried. What a mother, what a hero! She fought first with an indifferent husband, then with a lethal disease and finally, with her misunderstanding son. But she never gave up. My tears and love for her had no end. We sat there, just being in each other's company. I thought about Lama Yontan and immediately pledged that the purpose of my life would be to find joy for her. If not as a mother, she deserved it for being a great human being.

"I am not leaving you even for a minute now, Mom. I am sorry, you've been through such hardships and I did nothing to ease your pain or be by your side. All I was concerned about was my big ego and my own self," I told her.

She smiled. "It's not your fault, son. I should have told you this long ago." We hugged one more time and I felt like I had found my salvation.

I stayed with her that night at her hotel. I called Sasha over and the moment he saw me next to her in the lobby, he exclaimed, "Where is my friend Abhay?"

My smile was exuberant and loud and my best friend could see the difference instantly. He was very happy to see my mother, though he didn't feel the need to ask me anything. Perhaps that's the kind of connection everyone talks about. I considered myself extremely lucky to be with two people who understood me the most, and now, I had to prove that I valued them too. I told her about my history with Sasha. Sasha then asked, "Aunty why don't you join us on our return to Delhi? We will just stop by at Agra for a day. That's all. Besides, you can fill in for..." he stopped. I then briefly told her about our third friend Unnati and everything that had ensued.

After a good laugh, she said, "Thanks kids, but this trip is your thing. You must live it with each other only. I will see you in Delhi next week."

"Okay, at least be our model for Varanasi. Why don't you give us a good summary of this holy city for our movie? We don't have Unns to do it now," he asked me.

I brought my camera and focused on her. She smiled and said a few lines about the holy the city. For her, Varanasi was a second home. She had a wealth of information to share. She told Sasha, "Promise me that the first thing you will do after returning is to help Abhay move in with me!"

He smiled.

"Next, you have to bring Unnati around for dinner. Third, I will meet your and her parents and try to convince them about your alliance. And fourth, promise me you will find a girl like her for Abhay too."

Sasha replied, "Don't worry, aunty. He is the stud. I am just his side-kick."

We laughed.

"Bhai, did you not tell her about Jaisalmer's desert safari?> And that girl, Sakshi?"

"Shut up Sasha!" I hushed him and we laughed again. Having your mother around is something special. I felt so complete. Nobody can go back and make a new beginning, but anyone can start now and make a new ending.

Two brothers, one chic, and a *halwai* shop

We woke up at 5:30 a.m. I saw my mother sleep peacefully while Sasha and I slept on the floor. Her face seemed calm. I always believed that every person was a hero in his mind. Here was a person whose story would be heroic to everyone else, too!

Without saying anything, we slipped away from the room and went back to our lodge to pack up. The penultimate leg of our journey was to begin and the renewed energy that I carried after having met my mom meant that I could have spent another couple of months on the road, easily. But I didn't want to. I wanted to go back and live the city life that I knew best. There were no fears about it now. There was nothing to run away from. I had so much to do for her and for myself. I eagerly looked forward to returning home every evening to find her waiting for me, to discuss my day and to talk about our feelings. Unnati was right. We men need a woman around us all the time for our sanity.

Sasha was eager to go back too, foe his own reasons. As we left Varanasi, he confessed, "You know, Ab, this little period of being away from her is getting worse. I wasn't missing her this badly even when we drove from Goa to the south."

"Yeah, that's because she was still in this car then, dumbo!"

"You know what I mean, dude. Don't you? Shut up and listen. You are right about a quick date for our alliance. After meeting aunty, I feel more confident that our parents will agree. Have you thought of anything yet?" he asked.

"Actually, I have, but have to think it through. You have to fulfill two promises, remember?"

I slowed the car down to avoid a speed-breaker. Uttar Pradesh highways had generously laid them out. I guess being a construction-contractor would be a sought-after business in this state.

Agra was quite far. It was around 600 kilometers and a good ten hours away. We had tried to cover as much distance as we could and drove ferociously. But at the fag end of a long tour, we decided to take it easy and stop on the way at a few of UP's famous cities. Our first stop was for lunch at Allahabad. We went near legendary actor Amitabh Bachhan's childhood home on Clive Road, Civil Lines, and chose to settle down at a posh-looking cafe. It was euphoric to stare at an old bungalow that once housed the hero. I guess sitting at such a landmark called for inspiring the hidden hero in my friend, too. But first I had to let him talk to his girl.

"Call her, Sasha," I said, twirling the spoon in my coffee.

"Unnati? Told you! Her folks are mad at me and won't let her answer my call."

"Give me her sister Timki's number!" Sasha gave it to me and I called her. "Hi Timki! This is Abhay. Unnati's friend."

"I know who you are, you are Sashank's friend too, right?" she thundered.

"Yeah. Listen that's not why I called."

She listened and waited for my response, so I continued, "You would know that your didi is the star of my movie. You know that, don't you? Our producers in Mumbai are very impressed with her work so far. They might offer her a couple of other projects. She's going to be this huge thing!" I paused to sigh, for dramatic effect. "And you, lucky you, you'd be the star-sister in the Delhi circuit soon. Man, I remember we met briefly once at your house.

I suggest you should start accompanying her to these producers' offices. Who knows?" I sighed again. "Anyway. Is she around? I need to give her a message from Bingo!" I said.

"Bingo who?"

"Oh! Our producers, don't you know? Bingo Productions? Suraj..."

"Oh my gawd! Yes of course. I'll just her give her the phone. Listen, don't tell anyone that you called me, okay? And do meet me when you guys are back in Delhi," she said excited. There is this thing about stardom that can excite corpses too. Unnati came on the phone.

"Hi Sasha, how are you my coochie?" she whispered.

"Coochie? Ha! So you are dying to speak to him only, I see!" I teased her.

"Ab! No, it's great to hear your voice finally. I miss you guys. And damn this leg, I want to be in that car right now!" she said with the usual spark in her voice.

"Yeah, we miss you too, Unns. Here, talk to your lover-boy. See you soon!" I handed over the phone to him.

"Hi baby!" he turned mushy. Guys, committed ones, those who have proposed marriage, have their own distinctive style.

"Yes, we are on the way to Agra. We've made a small detour to Allahabad now actually. Big news? Well, two of them. We met a famous Buddhist teacher who gave us both a fresh lease of life. Yeah, I mean, spiritually," he said. I smiled and got back to my coffee. "The second, is even bigger... Ab met his mom in Varanasi... Yeah! I am not lying... Oh he is very happy about it... He has decided he will live with her once our trip is over... Yeah, wait one sec!" He gave me the phone again.

"Yeah, Unns. You heard it right. I swear I was thinking about you, grandma... You were right... Okay, no shouting on the phone! You are supposed to be sick... All right, not sick but at least behave! Otherwise your parents or your Timki will hear you... Here, talk to him!"

I left them on their own and went to the counter and looked at their exhaustive menu that hung behind. It was painted in the colors of the rainbow. Each color had some dish or the other made out of a common ingredient. White had all things made from eggs. Red had all dishes out of tomatoes, etc. It was quite innovative. And then it struck me. I came back to my seat, running, and asked Sasha to hang up quickly.

I put a finger on my lips and asked him to disconnect. When he didn't, I snatched the phone and said, "Bye Unnati, see you in Delhi this weekend." He shoved his middle finger in the air.

"Sasha! I have it!"

He looked disinterested but said, "What?"

"You only remember half of your promise. I also asked you to set up your halwai shop. Hear me out. Your wedding date is decided. It will be the same date as the opening of your shop."

"Yes, and my parents will hang me outside that same shop!"

"Hush! You have to simplify yourself. If you cannot handle that counter, then you just can't. Don't mind me saying this, but auto-parts? I mean, who cares how the car runs? Nobody thinks about the wiper or the headlight when driving, right?"

"Actually, we trade with the ancillary ones. Like spark plugs, fan belts, hammer unions and stuff," he corrected. "Okay, okay. I get it. I will do something else. But halwai shop? You know how difficult it is, don't you?"

"What? Society?"

"Exactly!" He became engaged, because it was his passion.

"Sasha, as far as I know, food is in the marrow of your bones! Look, this profession may not be the staircase to societal bliss, but who cares? Let go of that image! You have to do it. All your life."

"What if you'd not be collecting payments in thousands or lakhs behind that counter? Here, your bill will be hundred rupees earned after making someone truly happy and rub his stomach with fulfillment. You love your food so much that I can't imagine you serving anyone a bad portion ever. That's what counts. Besides, someday, you might become a halwai-chain owner, who knows."

"You're talking like Unnati now. Bhai, it's not that simple. Forget respect for a second. What about making ends meet?" he reasoned.

"For that, my friend, yours will be a revolutionary halwai shop, serving the best of the best street foods of India. It will employ people from states that we've visited – local culinary experts dishing out popular items of their cuisine that represent their region. Like that chef in Madurai. I am sure you can pay him a lot more in Delhi, won't you? What else does a regular halwai serve in Delhi? Answer me!"

"Samosa, jalebi and some mithai. What else?" he said.

"Yeah, and add to it some litti-chokha from Bihar, jalebi and poha from MP, dabeli from Gujarat, egg rolls from Kolkata, Rajasthan's kachori and sambhar-vada from Chennai!" I beamed.

"And that's not all. Sweets, you said? So how about Agra's petha, Bengal's rasgulla and mishti doi, Mysore pak, shrikhand and laddu!"

He was buying into it now.

"Yeah!" I exclaimed.

"All under one roof! Sounds like a brilliant business idea, Ab!" His eyes sparked.

But he quickly added, "It isn't going to be easy. So many chefs will mean so many salaries to pay, for such inexpensive halwai items."

"I know it will not be easy, Bhai. But if you put your heart into it, you will succeed, I know." I coaxed him.

"What about my parents? My uncles? They are all counting on me."

"That's where you have to use Lama's third advice of being grateful. Show them your gratitude for teaching you, for raising you so well and for helping you become the individual that you are. Talk to them of your distinctiveness, which came from their values and upbringing. I am sure they will agree. Parents love their children unconditionally. I too eventually found out that I was wrong about them, isn't it?"

He settled and thought for a minute, "Ab, will you join me?"

"What do you mean?"

"I can't do it alone. I will convince them, but I can't run such a venture alone. I am not good in administration. Will you help me?" He sounded serious.

I had too much stuff of my own to figure out. He added, "At least in setting it up initially?"

"Yeah! You came on this trip for me, and to help me make this movie. Can't I do this much for you?" I hi-fived him.

Having me by his side gave him confidence, and as we gulped our food quickly, he said, "I am thinking of opening this 'All-India-Halwai' with its first shop near our existing counters in Chawri Bazar. It's a busy market after all!"

"Great name!" We returned to the car with huge smiles.

Life seemed to be on such an upward move ever since Bodhgaya. Gautam Buddha could truly be credited for starting a spiritual movement from that place, and we were its latest beneficiaries. We sang songs, laughed to our hearts' content at the silliest of jokes and truly had the drive of our lives from Allahabad to Kanpur, where we stayed overnight. We then went further from Kanpur to Agra the next day.

Agra was our last destination and the symbol of our country to the world. The Taj Mahal is one of the Seven Wonders of the World and is an epitome of architecture and history, of creativity, of grandeur and of love. Mughal Emperor Shah Jahan had gotten it built in fond remembrance of his wife. This in itself was a reason for passionate souls all over the world to pay a visit. It was nothing new for us, as natives of Delhi. It was done to death – but it still continued to charm us every time we visited. This time, though, it was extra special. Against all odds, we had special permission to shoot at night, under the full moon in its full glory. Then, it was to be our last stop before we headed home after seventy days on the road.

We reached the Taj Mahal late in the evening and held our special VIP passes a little snobbishly. There was a mixed crowd of around fifty for that special sighting. Once inside, I quickly set up my camera, while Sasha stood watching the moonlight bask down on Taj Mahal slowly. I told him, "Call Unnati, I want her to give some live feed!" He hesitated but tried nevertheless, because it was late in the night. Luckily she picked after just a ring.

I told her, "Unns, this is your RJ moment! You don't have a visual. But you still have to describe whatever is happening here with your imagination. If it isn't good enough, we will edit it out. But you are the queen of impromptu and an amateur recorded movie can come across best on a live feed. So please say something kickass!"

She started, "It doesn't matter what time you look at the Taj. Emperor Shah Jahan used to look at it day and night and never get bored or tired of it. It is that beautiful a monument. But looking at the Taj on a silent night with the full moon above is a sight that you carry to your deathbed. Yes, you go out of here and stalk people with stories of this dazzling view. When rays of the moon light up the entire monument and paint it in a faint silver glow, you can almost imagine Shah Jahan holding hands of his beloved Mumtaz sitting right in front of it. Though the entire experience is all of thirty minutes, you sense a stillness of time as you start losing your soul to the mirage of its beauty. If anyone ever wants to test the purity of their love, they must visit the Taj Mahal by night. Cynics might say that there is nothing to see and that it's a waste of money, but it is a matter of perspective. When you come out of the compound, you will start valuing your senses more than ever."

When she finished, we were stunned, still staring at the Taj. I scratched my head and wondered why she had remained an Assistant RJ all this while. I looked at Sasha, but saw that his eyes were moist and he still hadn't disconnected the call. Then he told her, "Start preparing Unnati. We are getting married soon."

"I know that, coochie. Hey… are you crying? Why?" she asked with concern. He looked at me. I came close and signaled a three followed by one, and then rolled my hand anti-clockwise to him.

He said, "We are getting married on the 31st of the next month. It is final. Just start your preparations and wait for me, my Mumtaz Mahal!"

New ending, or
new beginning...

It was like a dream to me. I thought that somebody would wake me up and that I'd be on my bed, restless, as I was on the eve of the start of our journey from Delhi. There was so much to think of when we started out. We wondered how things would unfold and whether or not we would have it in us to finish the trip. Now, we had done it! The bond of search was coming to its end. Getting up late in the morning for that final drive back to Delhi, there was so much on my mind. Technically, the journey was over. The movie shoot had ended. In three hours, our marathon journey of seventy-one days would be over. There was so much to ponder upon. So far we had transgressed. Yet at the end, it all looked so complete.

"The heavens too are ready to welcome us. Look at that dark sky!" Sasha excitedly told me as we stepped out of the hotel lobby. We quickly drove to Panchhi Petha shop on the outskirts of the city to get some of Agra's famous pethas packed. I noticed Sasha talking with extra interest to one of the waiters behind those counters, and trying to get as much information about the kitchen as possible. To me, this confirmed that the All India Halwai Shop would be for real. Just as we placed our package in the car, heaven's gates opened and it started raining heavily. "I don't believe this! Rains in early June!" I whined.

Sasha stepped back and started dancing like a peacock welcoming the rain, or rather a bull thumping in the water. The smile on his face got bigger and he closed his eyes and looked up at the sky as he danced. I looked at him, getting wet, and after a minute, joined him in that jig. People standing outside their shops, under little sheds, watched us dance. Some passers-by with umbrellas stopped and wondered if evil spirits had captured us. We rocked like carefree bums, and everyone around had no idea of our joy, and how God had chosen to mark our special occasion.

"That was fun, Sasha! We must do it whenever it rains back home," I told him, as we finally got back into our car. It was still raining cats and dogs outside. He smiled and started the engine. The drive was pretty smooth even through loud thunderstorms and the heavy rain. Roads were slippery because of the heavy downpour. I asked him to drive slowly, though he didn't pay too much attention.

The lanes were pretty empty, as the highway had opened just last week as per tabloids. After a while, we saw some huge yellow police barricades. There were four policemen wearing raincoats and holding torches in their hands. We slowed our car when we reached them. One of them came running to Sasha's side and asked him to open the window.

"What are you guys doing here?" he asked us harshly.

Sasha said, irritated, "Driving. What else can people do on a highway?"

"Trying to be a hero! Asshole! Park your car on a side and get down!" he roared.

I pitched in, "Sir, forgive him. We are going back to Delhi. We are moviemakers and had come to shoot in UP. Is there something wrong?" I asked.

Another cop joined them by then. "This highway isn't open to the general public yet. We are wondering how you got entry. Didn't those toll-keepers stop you? Idiots! Anyway, park on the side and pay the penalty. You will have to reverse and go back."

I pleaded with him. "Sir, it's raining so heavily. Why are you making us pay the price for the tollbooth's mistake? We have been away for two months from home, because of this shooting. We aren't aware of the rules yet. Please forgive us and let us pass."

He shook his head and came towards my side. By this time, the other two had also joined him and soon there were two policemen on either side of the car. I knew we had no option but to talk to them nicely and you know, try to strike a little deal. That's what one expects from four policemen sitting in the middle of nowhere and under heavy rain. I told them, "Sir, can you get inside the car? We can talk here rather than getting wet."

The two of them got into the back seat while the other two stayed outside.

Once inside, I pleaded again. "Sirji, why bother collecting a fine and sending us all the way back? We had read in the newspaper that the highway is ready now. Please let us pass now, can we..." I stopped.

"Can we what?" he asked crudely.

"Can we not do something...you know...what I mean."

He laughed and looked at his companion. The other guy sitting behind Sasha brought out a knife and placed it on his neck and said, "Okay. So do one thing. Give us all the cash and possessions that you have."

"What the f..." Before I could finish, another knife came out. This time, the other guy held it to my throat and it was even bigger. "Don't try to do anything stupid."

I swear I could sense Sasha pee in his pants. I too had no balls to put up a fight of any sorts.

"Sir... we are backpackers...poor travellers... you can check us." I trembled while saying so.

"Earlier you said you were filmmakers, asshole! Now what happened? The movie got shelved or your sister got fucked by the producer so ran out of money!" he abused me badly and started laughing. He signaled to his other two chums and asked them to get inside too. Sasha and I shook in fear while these four hooligans took over the proceedings. They ripped every seat open, and every bag that we had and kept looking for money or valuables. Since we had very little cash left in real, they became angry when they found nothing.

"Rip their clothes apart! Let's see if they have any money hidden there or at least some jewelry on them!" the leader told the rest of them. They dragged us outside, tore off our shirts and jeans to find nothing except for a little gold chain that Sasha wore. Having taken our wallets already, they were still disappointed. Unluckily, they took it out on us and started trampling on us with their boots.

Lesson for everyone – please carry more cash/ valuables for prospective loot. If your assailants don't get enough booty, they take out their anger on you.

After having beaten us badly with blood spurting out and injuries, shoe-marks and swollen lumps everywhere on our bodies. they finally stopped. The leader was still sitting inside the car and came out with our number placards in his hand.

"What is this?" he asked placing his boot on Sasha's leg. I adjusted my jaw and checked my cheeks. Thankfully, there were no injuries on my face at least. The leader came and shouted at me again, "What are all these numbers for?"

"Sir... As I told you... We are poor... Moviemakers... We go to all villages... Of UP... Uttarakhand... Bihar... make movies... feature villagers experiences... to make them get noticed... their skills get showcased..." I spoke slowly due to the pain.

"I asked what these numbers are for!!"

"Each number denotes a village... so for example, the last number you will find is nine... This was the last village we went to... Kundol... near Agra..." I said again.

One of the robbers seemed interested. "I know where Kundol is. What did you do there?"

Sasha said, "They make excellent sugarcane juice!" and then mellowed down, due to the fear of being beaten up again. He spoke in a low tone, "We recorded some of its people making this juice... now when we go back, we will try to create awareness around it. Hopefully, one day, all sugarcane juice sold across India will be sourced from Kundol."

The leader was dismissive, "Fuck it, Hariya. They are talking nonsense."

"No, no sir! We are not lying. Hariya, sir, I will show you the video we made. Abhay, get it!" Sasha sat with his hands folded. I had no clue what he was talking about, but got it nevertheless. Sasha snatched it from me and rewound it. It had stopped raining and Sasha miraculously remembered our five-minute stop before Agra for a glass of juice from a roadside handcart. I don't know what made me record it. He played that video for Hariya. Sasha added, "This is just little raw footage, it will be very dramatic after editing and with background score. Of course, Kundol will be acknowledged in it."

Hariya and the others looked at it with great interest. They admired a poor, stick-like fellow, crushing sugarcanes in a hand-run machine, and pouring out juice for us. They recounted the spot where the shoot had happened and were now buying into our story. They whispered something to each other and then said, "Listen boys, you are doing good job. Go, you are free to go. Here, take your cameras and suitcase too."

We couldn't believe what we heard. Not to give them a moment to change their minds, I quickly brought out a pair of jeans and another shirt from my bag. I saw their leader shaking his head and heard him shout at his men, saying, "Now, get your wives married to them and offer yourself as dowry! Bunch of losers you are."

They paid no heed to him. We got to our feet and got into the car, when the leader shouted again, "Oye! Government's pension scheme gets over here. My men are emotional fools, not me. You won't get this car back. Now buzz off!"

"But sir..." I pleaded. He glared with his big red eyes and I stepped back. He asked his guys to get into the car and took the driver's seat. One of them removed the barricades, and within seconds, the car zoomed out of sight.

❖

"What stories you cook, Ab!" Sasha said. I wondered who had really twisted it, but it wasn't important.

"At least they spared our life..." he added.

I gave him a look. "Yeah? Let's celebrate! They took everything. How do we go back now? They took our phones too!"

Sasha put his hand on my shoulder. This was not how I could ever foresee our journey's end. This road trip continued to surprise us at every turn.

❖

After standing on an empty Yamuna Expressway for a good hour-and-a-half, we were spotted by an elderly couple driving at a snail's pace in an old ambassador. They agreed to hear us out and gave us a lift till Delhi.

Uncle asked me, "Won't you go to the police, boys? I think the nearest police station should be behind us."

I told him, "We are too exhausted after this, uncle! We will figure it out after we reach Delhi."

The lady gave us water and some bandages as well. We thanked them and I requested her to let me use her phone. I remembered Tanya's number by heart and called her to tell her about everything that had happened. I should have called Mom too, but I didn't want to worry her. Sasha then called Unnati to tell her what had happened.

Sasha said, "Our journey will end as planned. We will go to Jama Masjid tonight, have a meal in the bylanes and then go home."

I could totally relate to him, even though the old couple looked puzzled. The lady gave us some money for our journey home after dropping us at Anand Vihar. We thanked them and bade them goodbye.

❧

Sitting inside Lucky autorikshaw that we took from Anand Vihar Metro Station to Jama Masjid, we were finally breathing the air we had left behind us. It was a mix of pollution, dirt and humidity post-rain, but it was the air we recognized instantly. You can go anywhere, travel to the best of places, but home is home. Given the fact that we had lost possession of our car (not technically ours, but who knows our producer might just send its bill) and also our dignity being beaten up by a bunch of crooks; it wasn't exactly a happy homecoming. But once Delhi's air made way through my nose past my lungs and into the body, I forgot everything. All hardships from day one till the afternoon vanished just like that.

The autorikshaw stopped a little away from Jama Masjid's gate. "One thousand rupees," he announced.

"Oye, we are locals! What is the meter rate?" Sasha barked at him. He still had a lot of agony inside him, and was looking for a vent-out. Luckily, the auto guy took him on and became his target. After a lot of arguing, we finally paid him what he deserved and got out to stretch ourselves. After taking a short walk, we became one with our home-city again in a matter of minutes. The bazaar was crowded as it was late evening, and the lingo being spoken around was like old Hindi music to our ears. Too tired to titter around, we decided to go straight for a meal at Karim's.

Those familiar with the Delhi food-scene have most definitely heard of Karim's near Jama Masjid. Even the vegetarians have, although the place is famous for its non-vegetarian fare. I have dined there atleast a hundred times myself (I may be exaggerating, but hey, I just got beaten up a few hours back!) and Sasha would have never bothered to count. Although it was a weekend, we managed to get a table in a secluded corner in the otherwise busy set-up.

"Tandoori raan?" Sasha looked at me without even looking at the menu. Usually it takes about an hour or so for this delicacy to be prepared. But looking at the rush, I had my doubts that they'd be able to serve it. However, to our surprise, one after another, a server started bringing some of their mouth-watering dishes to our table. And then it was there, the tandoori raan, exquisite and elaborate!

"But we haven't even ordered yet?" I asked him in surprise.

The steward said, "Sir, I have your order pre-booked with me."

"By who?" Sasha asked him.

"Mobile-age sirji. Your order was placed with us yesterday and your picture was sent on WhatsApp. You guys famous? Also, entire bill has been paid already. Enjoy your food, sir. I will bring the main course whenever you are ready." and he went away.

"Who paid it?" I gave a puzzled look to Sasha who was busy digging into the food.

"I did!" I turned around at hearing Unnati's voice. Sasha too stopped and stood up flabbergasted. She walked inside slowly with the help of a walking stick and her left shoulder supported by another lady. It was Tanya!

"Surprise surprise!" Tanya shouted enthusiastically. We were truly surprised. There were hugs followed by peals of laughter and Karim's staff knew something unusual was going on in that little dining room.

"So good to see you, Unns! But you shouldn't have. Is your leg okay?" Sasha asked her as we settled down.

"It's not that bad, just a hairline fracture. Yeah I should've rested and yeah it could get worse and blah blah – who cares? How could I miss this moment! We all were looking forward to it badly, weren't we?" she smiled hugging her beau again. Tanya too was all smiles, though I felt guilty seeing her as I had not made any communication with her over the last week since Unnati's mishap. It was obvious she had found out everything already.

"Tanya, I am so sorry for not informing you about the accident," I confessed immediately. Having met Lama and my mother, I had decided never ever to stretch an apology again in life.

"Ah forget about it. It happens. This is your moment guys, enjoy it. Do we get beer here? Though this place looks a little tacky, doesn't it? You could've chosen a better venue..." she said in her usual upmarket way.

"Never mind. I am so happy to see you, alive. Look at you two, beaten up by goons in the afternoon and you're here for your ultimate moment rather than being at a doctor's! I must say there is more Bollywood in the blood of Delhites than that of the Mumbaikars!" We all laughed.

"Yeah, sorry about your car too." I shrugged.

"Abhay! Do you think it's easy to run or hide after robbing Suraj's car? He is one of the most connected and influential people of our country. The car has already been tracked down and the guilty will be behind bars before tomorrow morning. Your possessions will also be returned in a day or two. You guys don't bother about it." She put us at ease.

Sasha and I hi-fived each other and sighed in relief. We were happier about the fact that those bastards were caught. And no, Kundol's sugarcane juice isn't becoming the drink-of-India anytime soon.

"So tell me about the last few days?" Unnati asked. Without even waiting for an answer she asked again, "What made you so senti, Sasha? We can wait for the D-day for a while, can't we?"

"No we can't. Ab won't let us wait. I have made that vow to him. And besides, it will also be the date of opening of my new venture – All India Halwai Shop. I want to make it lucky by getting married on that very day." Sasha replied looking into her eyes. I could see his determination and was pleased. Unnati gave him a peck on his lips. I was cool with it. This probably meant I was completely over her, or had atleast accepted them as a made-for-each-other couple for life.

We told her some of the stories in detail and she heard them with great excitement. She also warned that convincing her parents wouldn't be the easiest thing to do. Even my mother may not be able to swing it in their favor as they thought of Abhay as an irresponsible person now.

"Love will make it happen, don't worry about it, Unns," Sasha announced.

Tanya entered again and said, "Yes guys, love will make it happen indeed. Here, eat this piece of bakra (goat) from me, all three of you. Fabulous job. You've made a great entry for this year's bakra series."

"Say it again?" I stopped eating, not sure what I had heard.

She shouted, "Bakra" and brought out that vintage bakra cap from the Cyrus Broacha MTV Bakra days from her bag and put it on my head. My mind stopped thinking for a second.

She laughed, "What? Come on, you didn't have a clue? Not for a second? This was for the all new episodes of Bakra. Why would Bingo produce a handycam-shot travel film? You knew it didn't have much meat, didn't you?"

She started clapping while we three sat dumbstruck.

She added again, "Come on. It's not that you made this journey for us? You were on this road-trip anyway, and would have completed it one way or the other for your dream, right? Don't react like this, it will look great in our bakra-series on TV."

"T...that's...true, isn't it, Ab?" Sasha stammered and looked up at me. My eyes were red and if there were a butcher's knife around, I would have attacked Tanya.

Sensing my state, Unnati said, "Yes. Abhay had to edit the movie, make it commercially watchable and then send it across to producers to get it released. It didn't cross our mind earlier, but why would a reputed production house take it over midway just like this. We don't even have a track record." She too hung her head low while saying all this.

I was in no mood for food anymore. I felt stupid and exhausted and just wanted to go home. Suddenly Tanya burst out laughing. She held her stomach as she laughed wildly and almost fell to the floor. Frankly, I had no energy left for her histrionics.

"Sorry Abhay. You got so serious, otherwise I'd have stretched this joke a lot further. How can I spoil your special day for my fun? This is all for real. Just forget about the bakra thing, and be jubilant again."

"It wasn't funny!" I scrawled at her. Seeing my stiffness she dramatically held her ears and said, "Sorry sorry". Unnati and Sasha heaved a sigh of relief.

This movie meant a lot to me and this joke was really cruel. Tanya sat next to me and rubbed my shoulders. I returned her a smile. She said, "Okay, but guys, before I go, let me tell you some serious business. Abhay, this bakra-thing was unreal, but one important bit missing from your footage was Unnati's part over the last one week or so. I guess from the Sundarbans onwards."

"Yeah, but we will cover it up. She even gave voice-over for the Taj Mahal portion," Sasha spoke up.

"I know about it; I had taken all details from her on the way. But come on, this is a real movie. The audience will easily make out she's missing from sequences," she said. Sasha's face hung low.

"Guys, I am not saying that we are not releasing it. That decision is actually not in my hands. Big boss, Suraj himself calls the shots. And remember, he told Abhay during our meeting that the star of the movie is its unconventionality – three friends, two guys and one girl on a real road-trip and neither must pull out at any point of time. I don't know how he will judge this. I don't know how our creative team will look at it. I am sorry but all that is beyond any of us at this point of time at least."

"Tanya," I said and looked at her, "this is unconventional, because this is for real. One gets injured for real. We have all those sections recorded. She goes to the nearest airport and flies home. This is all for real. If anything, this just adds an edge to the experience for the viewers. Besides, Suraj also asked us to commercialize it. People want to see action, and this is reality-TV-action. Don't you think?"

"You talk sense, Abhay. That's why I guess Suraj agreed to back this project. Look, I am not getting hypercritical; I am just saying that they will take this into consideration. Anyway, we will meet up in Mumbai next week when you come to our edit studio," she said getting up and wishing us goodbye.

Before leaving she added, "Ab, I have a feeling that it will work out." She gave a parting smile. We all looked at each other. Nobody knew what was going to happen with the movie part.

Unnati asked, "At least we made a record for India Books, right? We did? I mean you did? I mean..." she went blank.

I didn't know what to say either.

"Chuck the worries for now, bhai. We will save it for later. At least our trip is over successfully and all three of us are alive, sitting here and feasting. What more do we want?" Sasha cajoled me.

Unnati added, "Yeah, and there was an added bonus that finally my Mr Right has proposed and we are going to get married next month. I know for sure that Ab has a hand in it, otherwise I know my coochie!"

"And I united with Mom. Not only that, I was finally able to get over my parents' divorce and years of emotional baggage that I had carried," I contributed, getting jolly again.

"Ab! Brother! Don'tmiss out the big news around my business. My halwai shop! Owner Sashank Gupta. My family and our extended circles will die of shock or enroll in a mental asylum when they come to know."

We laughed at the way he spoke. But he was right. Everyone who knew us would be dumbstruck when they would see us in our new lives, the foundation of which was the trip that had lasted seventy-one days.

The icing on the cake would be our movie being released. But as Lama had advised, we had to move away from attachments and expectations and embrace an attitude of gratitude for our times to come.

For that, Tanya and Suraj deserved thanks from us. Our dinner continued till midnight as we kept reminiscing over our trip and the interesting people that we had met.

We talked about Unnikrishnan, our first tour guide at Corbett who laid the stepping-stone for this roller-coaster ride. We talked about our incredible hosts in Ladakh, Dorjee and his wife Diki, and decided to write them a long letter. We laughed and made fun of the guy in Amritsar because of whom (Yes, in hindsight, he was at greater fault!) there was havoc at the border that day.

Sasha, the affable bastard that he is, couldn't help but bring Sakshi's name and they teased me by calling her Sakshi-bhabhi again and again. We recalled that stunt at Kanyakumari and how I had to hold the security guy at imaginary gunpoint.

We laughed at Sandeep – the Hyderabadi-foodie and HFJ's founder even though we decided to not show him in bad light in our final version. Finally, we spoke about Lama Yontan's session and the invaluable tips he gave us. One must follow his principles not only on a road trip or in a troubled situation, but also for the entire journey of life.

If you truly do that, no recording or movie is required. Your journey itself becomes your reward and your notions find their true colors.

www.ingramcontent.com/pod-product-compliance
Lightning Source LLC
Chambersburg PA
CBHW051656260626
47170CB00004B/1533